MISSION TO CATHAY

Illustrated by Peter Landa

MISSION
TO CATHAY

by Madeleine Polland

This edition published June 2000 by arrangement with the author.

Library of Congress Catalog Card Number 65-14019

ISBN 1-887840-21-4

For a catalog of Sonlight Curriculum materials for the home school, write:

Sonlight Curriculum, Ltd.
8042 South Grant Way
Littleton, CO 80122-2705
USA

Or e-mail: catalog@sonlight.com

For Fergus

1

Life seemed to have left the island of Macao, silent and sleeping under the moist heat of the Chinese summer; heat that pressed intolerably on the starved weariness of a boy who lay against the harbor wall, looking dully out over the flat, turgid sea.

With a sudden gesture, he roused himself and pulled at the ragged ends of his blue cotton coat, tying them tightly round his stomach and pulling viciously at the knots. Even that small effort exhausted him, but it helped to ease the hunger pain that nagged his mind as relentlessly as it nagged his empty stomach. Soon, he knew, he must eat or die, and he turned and looked defiantly along the hot stretch of the waterfront. In the worst heat of the day, the beggars of Macao had flung themselves down to sleep, in what shade they could find, and in the small coolness rising from the tepid sea. They were no more than heaps of fleshless rags, their small begging bowls forgotten beside them, for who would walk about, to give, at this hour in the high heat of the summer?

Desperately the boy gathered his knees up against his empty stomach. He would *not* beg. He did not know

what kept him from it, but he knew that he would rather die, and probably would, than become one of these heaps of rags, waking to drag themselves along at the hem of rich men's robes, whining for their pity. Somehow, somewhere, he would find some work to do. He had done so for long enough now; a few cash here, a few cash there; enough to buy a bowl of rice to stand between him and death. But now he had gone without food too long. His stomach tore at him and his head felt light and strange, and he needed to blink his eyes before he could see clearly.

At the moment, he could see clearly enough to know that the waterfront was gradually filling up, even though it was still the high heat of the day. People were beginning to gather; common people in their blue cotton suits, and better-dressed small merchants, and somewhere the shouts and jingling of the trotting palanquin-bearers of some rich man. There must be a ship due in.

Hope crept into his dull eyes. There was always the chance that someone might want something carried, although now he prayed that it might not be anything too large. He had not the strength. No rice, he thought foolishly, no strength. Carefully he stood up and steadied the swirling sea about his head, and when he could see properly he noticed that two men who were not Chinese had come on to the quay behind him. They were huge even for foreigners, and very hairy, as all these foreign barbarians were, priests or bonzes of some kind, dressed in ugly long black robes, and wide straw hats such as the Chinese wore themselves. He knew about them. They had a house and a temple in the town where they lived and worshiped their own strange god, and they always looked heavy and well fed, as if they had much rice. They may be meeting someone who would want something carried. It may even be that they needed a servant in their strange house. The ship was in sight now, sluggishly rounding the harbor point, and hopefully he edged up close to the foreigners.

The flat gray sea was as dead with the moist weight of the season as the gray sky that pressed above it, and between them the laden carrack from Goa drifted to her moorings, her idle sails collapsed against her mast and the lazy thrust of her bows barely moving the rubbish on the lifeless water. On board as she drew closer, the silence of heat lifted and the passengers were pushing and talking and laughing as they collected their bundles and boxes, lighthearted with relief to have made a safe passage through the dangerous seas from India. Alone and silent in the bows stood the tall, commanding figure of a man in a black soutane, and his disciplined patience gave no hint that his mind was as eager and excited as that of any chattering Chinese passenger. Although he stood quiet, his dark eyes could not race fast enough to take in all of the scene that was slowly drifting toward him.

China! At long, long last China, the ancient land of Cathay. True, it was only as yet the island of Macao that he had reached, and a few miles distant across the hazy sea the round, shadowy hills of the forbidden mainland still held their secrets to themselves. But Macao was the first step toward them, and he stared gratefully across the closing space of water at the huddle of shacks and houses that seemed to cling to the ground of the island. In the middle of the pushing crowd he looked at it all in silence, in his excitement alternately thanking his Christian God for bringing him so far, and begging Him to help him to go farther.

Some years previous to this late summer of 1583, the Jesuit Fathers had established their mission on this small offshore island of Macao, and one after another their priests had tried to journey on to the unknown and hostile mainland, to bring word of their own Christian Lord of Heaven to the blossoming valleys and the green rice fields and the jangled beauty of the bright pagodas.

But the Chinese authorities would not suffer the foreigners, those big-nosed hairy devils from barbarian lands who pushed in with their ignorance and crude manners, disturbing the fine civilization of their Flowery Kingdom. They laughed at the Jesuits and told them to be gone and take their Lord of Heaven with them. If the priests dared to linger, then the laughs faded quickly and there were threats of imprisonment and ugly death. At the time that Father Matteo Ricci stood in the bows of the carrack from Goa, staring hopefully across the sea to the Chinese hills, even the shortest visits to the mainland were forbidden by a new Viceroy in Kwangtung, and the hazy hills that he could see were as remote and inaccessible as if they were the mountains of the moon.

He dropped his eyes from them; they would be for the future. As soon as he turned to look down at the waterfront that had woken now to a crowded bustle, he cried aloud, his sober face lit up and his two arms raised in greeting.

"Father!" he cried, down on to the shore. "Father!" Below him the milling Chinese paused and looked up at the sound of his voice, and broad grins split their faces. They doubled up in delighted laughter to see another mad foreign devil in a black robe come to join the first two.

"Another hairy barbarian," they cried to each other.

"As savage as the others!"

"Listen to the shouting! And the man he greets is still distant the length of a good furrow!"

"Black foreign devil! See his big nose!"

Matteo Ricci only smiled at their laughter because he did not understand it, thinking only that they were amiable and friendly, as indeed they were. Impatiently he watched the two other priests who thrust their way up the gangplank through the grinning crowd to greet him on the deck, and he smiled at them when they reached him and gripped their hands; old friends long apart. Around them faces cracked with laughter, and small men in blue cotton clothes hugged themselves with delight to watch the uncouth greetings of the strangers.

"Michele!"

"Matteo! We are glad to welcome you!" Father Ricci met the warm greeting of his old friend, and the kind, quieter welcome of his new Superior.

"Father." They remembered themselves again, formality coming back after the first moments. "Father—which is your baggage?"

Matteo Ricci gestured around him. Space was clearing on the deck as the people poured ashore, and left in clear view were the piles of wooden crates and Italian woven baskets, and long, strange bundles wrapped in sacking.

"This," he said eagerly, and did not notice their faces. "And this, and this and this."

The other two priests stared, having themselves come

half across the world to Macao with all their worldly possession on their backs in one small bundle.

"All this?" asked the Superior in dismay, thinking of the small spaces of his Mission. "But Father—?" He viewed the crates and bundles, full of strange knobs and bumps, with straw peering through the sacking. "What is it all?"

Father Ricci looked at him, his own face now full of dismay.

"My instruments, Father. My clocks. My astrolabe. Tools and materials to make more clocks, and more mathematical instruments. I am a mathematician, good Father, this you know, and I was told that the Chinese love anything mechanical, the more complicated the better. I thought to reach them and interest them with some of my mechanisms!"

"Ah, yes. Do not distress yourself, Father. We will find room for them all, and as you say, it may be that they will win the Chinese heart."

He did not say that he himself had asked for Father Matteo Ricci for a reason quite apart from his mechanical marvels. He had asked for him because he had great dignity, and smooth, excellent manners. These things the Chinese valued above all else; correct behavior and good order in everything that was done. On this ground Father Ricci could meet them, where his more blunt and impatient friend had failed. And it would not hurt to let him have his clocks too, wherever they were to be put. He flicked his fingers to the Mission servants who

7

waited by the gangplank, and before Father Ricci could stop them a couple of the small men in blue cotton had seized his boxes and bundles, grinning at his frantic objections.

"Have care! Have care! My instruments!" He turned

from one to the other and they grinned their wide water-
melon grins and strung his precious boxes in great heaps
in the strings of their carrying poles. He pursued them
along the deck and down the gangplank, followed more
slowly by his smiling friends, and all the watching crowd

9

drew close to laugh at this new barbarian, who seemed even wilder and more curious than the others, shouting and waving his hands and covering his face.

"My clocks!" he cried. "Oh my clocks!" Covering his face did not stop him hearing the boxes bumped and thumped along the quay, and he took his hands down just in time to see a young boy whipping off with the last of his carefully packed bundles.

"No!" he shouted, and gathered up his robe to try and catch the child. The Chinese were delighted, all standing in his way with faces creased with laughter under their mushroom hats, for surely this foreigner was the funniest of all. Helpless he stopped, and from his greater height, watched over their heads to where the child disappeared with his most precious package of mathematical instruments. And a boy that did not look fit to be entrusted with a goat, with his cotton suit hanging in rags and fringes around his skinny body. His long, unkempt hair, of a strangely light brown, hung loose and ragged on his neck, not yet grown to the pig-tail of manhood. Even as he disappeared into the crowd and Father Ricci turned despairingly to look for the other priests, a voice spoke at his elbow.

"Father," it said. "Many respects and welcome to China. I am Philip, interpreter to the Fathers of the Mission. I am Portuguese, born in Macao." He bowed before the priest, pride and pleasure in his position glowing on his face, his brown curling hair packed away under a round cap. He spoke a mixture of Italian and bad Portuguese, easily understood by Father Ricci from the years he had spent in Goa. Eagerly the priest turned to someone who would understand him.

"My boxes," he said. "Philip, they are very valuable, and must be carefully handled. They are full of mechanisms."

Philip did not let his smooth face show that he had no idea what a mechanism was, but he bowed again helpfully.

"The other Fathers are following, to take you to the house of the Mission," he said, gesturing to where the two other priests made a more leisurely way through the crowd. "All the boxes are being cared for by the servants of the Mission," he added reassuringly.

Father Ricci had a sudden vision of a pair of starved ankles coming down like sticks below trousers of ragged blue.

"Even the small boy?" he asked sharply. Surely the Mission cares better than that for its servants?

Philip's bland face was puzzled.

"What boy does the Father mean? There is no small boy at the Mission."

"A boy of about twelve took one of my boxes."

The interpreter folded his hands and disclaimed responsibility.

"Here are the Fathers," he said, gesturing, and melted away himself into the thinning crowd.

Ricci found it hard to bear their calmness at his anxiety, assuring him as Philip had done that all the boxes would be at the Mission when he got there. He was unwilling to speak, his eyes combing the crowds for a sight of the small blue figure and his very precious bundle.

"My mathematical instruments," he said in the end, hesitantly, and now he did not know whether he was more troubled about them or about the boy. He knew that justice was harsh and summary in China, and theft was theft. Finally he got them to understand that it was a stranger who had taken his bundle; and there was no certainty at all that he would find it at the Mission.

"We had better go there at once," said the Superior. "At once."

They threaded their way through the crowded, narrow streets where the small shops laid out their goods in the open, almost in the very path of the passers-by. Hustlers and peddlers of all kinds drifted in the crowd, selling their wares from baskets slung across their shoulders on long poles; offering meat and fruit; melons and children's toys of bright painted wood; bread, and sweetmeats and small tasty tidbits to tempt the idle and the hungry, like sugared pomegranates or small dumplings dripping with hot, sweet-smelling syrup. The long streamers and ribands of the shop signs hung straight and brilliant in the still, hot air, and brightly painted arches spanned the streets, through which trotted the shouting, jingling carriers of wealthy merchants, their palanquins rich with gilt and scarlet and their curtains closely drawn against the curious. Noises and sights and smells such as he had never known before crowded on Father Ricci from every side; a bustle of color and raucous, busy living. Yet he could not keep his mind on the strange scene, nor on the cheerful conversation of the other priests, pointing out this and that. Against his will, he kept thinking of a thin, half-starved-looking young figure, scuttling away through the crowd, and he was reluctant to face what they might find, or might not find, when they reached the Mission.

It was a Chinese house, and not very large. Entry to the single court was through an arched gateway, above which the carved and painted Chinese characters had been taken away and replaced by a simple cross. Father Ricci followed the other two around the carved screen that was set across the gate, hiding the court from the street when it was open, and got a quick impression of simple, single-storied buildings with shallow, curving roofs, surrounding the court on three sides, their clawed pillars along veranda roofs gay with crimson and green and the gleam of gold. Small, beautiful trees stood here and there in tubs of gleaming porcelain, and in the middle of the court lay a small, tiled pool, a single lotus tree beside it, with the red hearts of the flowers open to the hazy sun.

His boxes were all piled on the tiles around the pool, but even before they turned around the snarling dragons of the screen, the three priests could hear the hubbub of argument and anger.

The anger boiled from the two Mission servants,

chattering furiously as they coiled the ropes which had bound the cases to their carrying poles. They were shouting together in quick, easy Chinese temper at the boy who stood impassively above the smallest bundle of all, which he had snatched and carried from the boat unasked, on his thin shoulders. Now he stood there in the soft heat of the sun beside the scarlet lotus, waiting as if he harbored such small strength as he might have left. His bony face was composed in indifference and dignity, as though the scolding servants were no concern of his, and his odd light brown hair was still dark with sweat around his forehead. The moment he saw the priests, his quiet broke. This was what he waited for, and he leaped across the court, bowing and gesticulating and talking all at once.

"Philip!" called Father Ruggieri, and Philip came quickly from one of the wings of the house. Understanding nothing, Father Ricci knew only a surge of pleasure that here was the boy, and here also was the precious bundle. Whatever he was, he was not a thief.

"What is it all about, Philip?" asked the Superior.

"Ah," said Philip, obviously wishing to have nothing to do with the whole Chinese squabble. "This young one says he has carried the heavy bundle, full of strange points and knobs, all the way from the boat on his own shoulders. This, he says, shows us that he is big and strong and could work as a servant in the Mission. He says he will bow down and worship our devil-god if you will take him as a servant, and give him only a mat to sleep on and rice to eat. The others say they do not want another servant in the Mission, above all one who would find his place by trickery."

The Superior made an impatient gesture.

"They are right," he said. "It cannot be done. If we do it for this one, we will soon have every starving child in Macao clamoring at our gates. You know that I would gladly feed them all, but we are too poor ourselves. We have little enough for our own work as it is. We cannot keep anybody else."

His normally strong and serene face was creased by this reminder of the poverty that dogged them in the Mission, slowing the pace of their work, and crippling their ambitions. In order to maintain it, and support the few priests who did its work, the Jesuits now ran several of the trading carracks between Macao and Goa. Lately there had been severe weather and terrible storms along the coast of India. Many of the carracks had been lost, and all their precious cargoes with them, and money was desperately short.

Philip shrugged at what the Superior said.

"That is what I tell the boy," he said indifferently. But Father Ricci was newly come, and did not know the terrible poverty of the priests of Macao. He did not see past the pathetic eagerness of the young face, and the sharpness of the bones which hunger had thrust up under the skin. For all their anxious eagerness, the dark eyes were dulled by near starvation. Over and above his pity, he was curiously attracted by some dignity in the

15

boy himself; some way of standing that set him apart from the two angry men behind him, and even from Philip, who boasted his Portuguese blood and some small measure of education. There was a look of good breeding in the starved face under the light brown hair.

Troubled by their heartlessness, Father Ricci opened his mouth to plead for the boy, and then remembered that he was only just arrived on this island and knew nothing. With an effort, he kept quiet.

"Give him a bowl of rice, Philip, and then send him away," said the Superior, and Philip took the boy distastefully by the ear to lead him off. Father Ricci could not stand the sudden crushed look on the child's face as he passed him, and he plunged into the deep pocket of his habit for the unfamiliar string of cash. As he thrust a few into the boy's hand, the child looked up, startled and grateful, and for one moment his eyes met the priest's as Philip hustled him away. "And try to tell him," the Superior called after them, "that there is more to being a Christian than being bought with a bowl of rice."

Father Ruggieri shook his head as his friend returned the string of cash to the depths of his pocket.

"Foolish, Matteo," he said. "Foolish." He shook his head again. "We do all we can for them in the name of God, but now he will tell his friends about the new simple foreigner, and we will have every beggar in Macao about our gates."

Father Ricci was unrepentant and a little puzzled.

"There was something about that boy, Michele."

"There's something about them all on this forsaken island," answered Michele, and his voice was dry. "They're hungry."

"Yes." Matteo Ricci was no stranger to the miseries of hunger. The mean streets of Goa had crawled with it, and it was not hunger that he saw in this boy. Firmly he put him out of his mind, and followed the other two priests into the small, pillared room set aside for a chapel, that they might all give thanks to God for his safe arrival within sight of Cathay.

2

It was the Superior's business to get Matteo Ricci permission to go into the mainland of China, and he set out to do his best, even though he had small hope of success. The business of learning Chinese was Matteo Ricci's own, and Father Ruggieri's, and they set about it the only way they could see, begging help from Philip and the servants, the shopkeepers, and the merchants of the town, and from anyone else who had the patience to speak with them. Father Ricci found it an intolerable frustration that he could not speak easily with these friendly people, and that the complex language took so long to learn, even for him, to whom any language came easily. It was so important; it was everything, in the matter of making contact with the Chinese.

But the patience and calmness for which he had been chosen on this mission did not forsake him in these tedious months, and he would walk tranquilly through the crowded streets and the bazaars, laying a hand on this and that and struggling to repeat what he was told. He could not resist dropping a few cash into begging bowls here and there, and he thought occasionally of the proud young boy in the Mission courtyard, who would not beg.

It was as if, giving to the beggars along the streets, he gave to the boy he had been unable to help. Had that boy now come down to a begging bowl along the roadside, or to starvation and death?

Gradually as the months passed Father Ricci forgot him, and with constant work, he managed to push away the bitter disappointment of the relentless refusals to allow him to enter the mainland of China.

During this long, trying time of waiting Matteo Ricci was bidden one day in the high summer to take some of his clocks to the pavilions of a local Mandarin, who was interested in such things. Philip was away from the Mission, but Father Ricci took courage and said he would go alone. He knew enough characters now, he thought, to be able to speak a little, and he set out in high spirits with two servants behind him, carrying the precious clocks. It was his first important chance to talk with the noble class of China, whom he wished above all to contact, as they would lead their people.

"Why did you not tell us, Philip?" he cried on his return, his face now dark with anger and disappointment. He had lost all his customary dignity and raged at Philip from the moment he came through the gates. "Why did you not tell us?"

Philip quivered with fright, his whiskers drooping and his long face shaking.

"Tell you what, Father? Tell you what?"

"Why did you not tell us that the Chinese you have been teaching us is the Chinese of the coolies and the shopkeepers! Why did you not tell us that there were two ways of speaking in this country!" He turned to the other priest, despair on his face. "We have learned nothing, Michele, nothing! Nothing for all our work, except how to bid a coolie gather up our bundles! In the kind of house I visited today, another language is needed; the Chinese of the Mandarins, that the educated people speak, and we have none of it. They were too courteous to laugh at me today, with my poor efforts in a coolie's tongue, but I could see the contempt in their eyes behind their fans! Michele, we must start work all over again, and who—who will be able to teach us Mandarin?"

In the days that followed Father Ricci came close to despair that between the lack of proper language and the hostility of the authorities, he would never set foot in China. Philip tried to comfort him, telling him that all the Scholars understood ordinary Cantonese, since they needed to speak it to their servants. He did not argue, but he knew this was useless. He must not come with his great message from the West, and try to spread it in the language of the poor. The Mandarins would only laugh behind their fans and send him packing. China seemed more remote and inaccessible than ever.

Sadly he stood with Philip one day on the waterfront, in the cool days of the year soon after the Christian Christmas, and just before the Chinese New Year. In silence he watched the trading junk with its square sail heading for Canton, and wondered bleakly if he would ever go with it. Refusals of permission to travel had been even more curt and abrupt than before. He shook himself from useless fretting and began speaking in labored Chinese with Philip. He was no longer troubled or embarrassed by the spurts of laughter around him every time he opened his mouth; laughter was friendly. This time, however, he could not go on speaking for the mirth that came from behind him, peal after infectious peal of it, so that a grin crept over his own face and he turned around. Doubled up at the quay wall, holding his stomach against his laughter, was the boy who had snatched his box on his first evening in Macao, and begged for work in the Mission.

Father Ricci looked at him with a strange start of pleasure, but his smile faded, seeing the young frame now little more than a skeleton, the strange brown hair hanging lifeless about a face whose starving planes were not hidden by the flush of laughter. What a people, he thought, that they will die of hunger even as they laugh!

"Ask him," he said to Philip, not trusting his own Chinese. "Ask him if he has seen me before."

"Yes," the interpreter said when he had spoken. "The boy remembers you as one of the black bonzes from the house of foreign devils."

"And where has he been since I saw him then?"

Philip spoke to the boy, who chattered rapidly, and the man creased his face and had to ask him to repeat what he said.

"He has had the sickness," he said then.

Cholera had ravaged Macao in the late autumn. No wonder the boy was like a walking bundle of bones. The priest turned in kindness and tried to speak himself, but the gaunt young face only quivered again and dissolved into helpless laughter, while the boy struggled at the same time to bow his head, his hands in his tattered sleeves, in the position of respect due to an elder who was speaking. Father Ricci could not help smiling back.

There was an open cheerfulness in the boy's face that took all the rudeness from his laughter.

"He finds you even funnier," Philip said, and there was a surprised and resentful tone in his voice, "because he does not speak the Chinese that you speak."

"What then does he speak?"

"I do not understand it, since he is a beggar, and there is much Cantonese mixed with it—but this boy speaks the pure Chinese that you Fathers wish to learn. He speaks the Chinese of the Mandarins; the language of the Scholars."

The boy straightened himself, with his odd, fierce dignity, and bowed again. His face was now solemn, closed in cool politeness. The priest on the other hand was growing unusually excited.

"Ask him who taught him to speak thus? Who taught him Mandarin?"

Philip spoke, although obviously unwilling to continue this conversation with a tattered beggar.

"Who taught you, unworthy one," he asked condescendingly, "to speak the Mandarin tongue?"

The boy looked only at the priest.

"I do not know," he said, slowly and carefully, in common Cantonese, so that the Jesuit would understand him.

"What matter where he learned it!" Father Ricci cried. "If he can speak it, we can listen and learn." But he could not help a sharp curiosity as to where this leggy, starving child had come by the language of the nobles of China. There was also this strange, quiet dignity about him, although there was always the feeling that the solemn face and the dark eyes would light quickly to a grin.

"Ask him if he has a home," the priest said then, and Philip looked at him as if he had taken leave of his senses. What beggar in Macao had a home, other than if he could find the shelter of a wall, or the cold stones of some abandoned temple!

"Ask him."

Contemptuously, Philip asked, and the boy shrugged again.

"Parents? Family? Master?"

All the same hopeless shrug.

"That is excellent!" The Chinese boy stared at Father Ricci's flood of delighted Italian. Because he could understand nothing, interest left him, and his exhaustion was clear in the pale bony face and the dull eyes.

"We will take him home with us, Philip! He can talk and we will listen to him. He will teach us Mandarin." He laid a hand on Philip's shoulder to calm the man's affronted dark face. "He can help us all."

Philip looked only half convinced.

"As the Father says," he said coolly, and spoke to the boy as condescendingly as if it were he who offered him a home. As the child understood, the dull face lightened until a beaming smile split it almost from ear to ear, and he gazed a long moment incredulously at the Jesuit. Then his hands went into his sleeve ends and he bowed and bowed again so low that all the priest could see was the brown hair fringed on his skinny neck. All the time he poured out a torrent of light, gasping Chinese.

"What does he say, Philip?" Father Ricci looked at the formal bows and reflected that someone had taught this boy more than Mandarin when he was small. "What does he say?"

Philip pulled at his long mustache.

"He says," he said sardonically, "that he will behave himself in the exalted house of his new foreign masters."

"His name?" Father Ricci asked then, and the man passed on the question.

The boy frowned momentarily as if the query troubled him, and then he shrugged and grinned again.

"Boy?" he said in Chinese, and with that the Jesuit had to be content.

They took him as a servant into the Mission, the boy with no name and no home and no family, and he settled down there as calmly as if he felt he had reached the one place where he belonged.

"Tell me something, Boy," the priest said curiously, as they sat together one day on the bright tiles that edged the parapet of the pool. The Festival of Ming Ching was close at hand, the Chinese Festival of Spring, and even on the crowded island of Macao where no crop grew and no field was tilled, the air was alive with the fresh urgency of the young season. The town beyond the Mission walls hummed with a sharper note, and the leaves of the lotus were beginning to unfurl in the soft, clear air.

"Tell me, Boy," he said, struggling to use the small number of Mandarin characters he had mastered and to imitate the boy's clear, beautiful tones. "Tell me of yourself. Why do you have no name, no home, no family?" He was puzzled. Everyone in China was so proud of his family.

The boy gave his characteristic quick shrug, and with it a doubtful and apologetic smile. He moved a thoughtful finger to disturb the pale goldfish floating in the pool.

"No name, no home, no family." He echoed the words, but kept his eyes on the broken ripples of water, as if ashamed that this was all the answer that he could give to this revered Father. "That is how it is, honored Father."

Father Ricci thought his questions might be at fault. He called Philip and asked him to question the boy further.

Distastefully, Philip obeyed.

"He says he remembers no home or family of his own. He knew life only in the house of a rich merchant where he was a slave. This man was very cruel to him, and when he sailed back to China to live, the boy slipped away as he was boarding his boat at the quay. That was the summer of last year and he has been living on the streets of Macao since then."

Father Ricci looked at the anxious face.

"But where would he come from? A slave, even, must come from somewhere."

Philip shrugged indifferently.

26

"He would have been sold by his parents as a baby. They must have been very poor indeed. It is the lowest disgrace for Chinese to sell a boy child. Usually they sell only girls, for which they do not care very much."

The boy was listening to every word, and now he began fumbling eagerly in the torn neck of his coat, his anxious fingers fishing up a silver chain with a small flat medallion on the end of it. Philip looked surprised, and took it from him, turning it over curiously.

"What is it?" asked the priest, and took it in his turn. On one side was a date and on the other the Chinese symbol for good luck.

"It is his birth chain," Philip answered, puzzled. "And it is a very good and valuable one. This shows he did not belong to a poor family in the beginning. No matter how poor they grew," he added, "this is one thing they would never sell, nor would anyone steal it from him, for the evil luck of such an act would be so great that they would not dare. But what puzzles me is his birth date is on it and the charm for good luck but there is nothing about his family. This is unusual."

The priest handed back the precious silver chain, and as the boy slipped it over his neck, he burst out again into a torrent of talk to Philip.

"He is troubled," the interpreter translated indifferently, "for it is the most shaming thing for a Chinese to have to admit he has no family. There is little worse that can be said about him. The boy begs the Father to know that in spite of this, he is good and honest, and begs him not to send him away."

The priest looked back at the odd dignity of the boy who stood now, silent, with his hands in his sleeves, head bent while he waited for his answer.

"Tell him," said Father Ricci gently, "that I am sure he is all he says he is, and we will not send him away. And tell him also," he added, "that now that he lives with us, he belongs as we all do to the great Family of the Lord of Heaven which we worship."

Philip told him, catching for the moment a little of the priest's gentleness, and Father Ricci had to lean over and disturb the fish again, for he could not look at the brimming pride in the boy's face, so close to unmanly tears that would have shamed him.

"Go now, Boy," he said, "and help the servants."

By now Father Ricci had been six months in Macao, and in spite of constant pleas he could not get permission to enter the Chinese mainland. As best he could, he occupied himself with his language study, with his clocks and timepieces and mathematical instruments for working out heights and distances and the movements of the stars. All these mechanical marvels filled the Chinese with respect that was almost worship, for they deeply loved anything mechanical, especially if it made loud noises like the striking clocks. By now, word had spread through all Macao that one of the black foreign devils had a room full of these devices, loud with ticking and clicking and striking, and the whir of revolving wheels. Distinguished Chinese came, led by their gongs and drums and trumpets and processions of servants, to stare at these devices with awe and respect. They went away to talk over their scented tea of all the strange things they had seen, and in time word spread even on to the mainland of this hairy foreign devil in the black robe, with his room full of ticking machinery.

In this way the damp, exhausting summer months passed, heavy with the hum of cicadas and laden with the perfumes of the flowers blazing in colored tubs around the court. The heat died and the hills of distant China grew brown and withered. The junks sliding into Macao were laden with the grass cut from their dry slopes for winter fuel for the island, and still every answer for Father Ricci that came from the mainland was a refusal. Foreign priests would not be allowed to enter Cathay.

Patience grew very difficult. Increasingly he would leave his littered table to go and stand at the latticed wall of the garden, staring out across the darkening sea toward the far hills. Was this all that he was ever going to see of China? Would he never get closer to this vast, challenging land with all its uncounted souls? Had God no use for China, that He would not answer his prayers to be allowed to go there?

He was standing at this spot when the boy came to him one evening at dusk, his eyes wide and blazing with excitement. But from his chittering talk, all that Father Ricci gathered was that his Superior wished to see him.

Softly he came through the house and out into the court behind the other two priests, who did not hear him come.

There was excitement of some kind in the air. Torchlight blazed in the dark water of the pool and the wide-eyed servants peered curiously from the shadows. As far as Father Ricci could see there was no cause for the excitement; only one stranger in the court, and he a common soldier, not even an officer, quite ordinary except that it was a little early for his long quilted coat, worn as if he might be still traveling when the weather grew cold. There was a strange, restless silence, as if the group had all said everything they had to say, and were now waiting. What were they waiting for? Was there danger of some kind?

As always, the boy's manners were perfect, no matter what was afoot, bowing before the Superior, hands in sleeves, and showing by the merest flicker of his eyes that his master was behind him in the shadows. The Superior turned, and there was a letter in his hands. It was Matteo Ricci they had all been waiting for.

"Matteo," he said, using his Christian name. "Matteo." His voice was a little hoarse. "God is good. This soldier comes from the town of Siuching, one hundred miles inland in the province of Canton. It seems that the Governor there, a Mandarin called Wang P'an, has heard of your fame as a clockmaker and a mathematician. This interests him, and he invites you, Matteo, to Siuching, and speaks hopefully of land where you may build. The soldier is here to escort you safely to him. Matteo, my son, with God's good help, you are in China."

The boy did not move from his polite position, nor did he raise his head, but in the uncertain torchlight, his brown face was creased with sudden puzzlement.

"Siuching," he whispered to himself, as if he did not understand what the name meant to him. "Siuching."

Father Ricci echoed him.

"Siuching," he said, but he could place a meaning on the name. For the greater glory of God, it would be the site of the first Christian Church in China.

3

There was much to be done in preparation for the jour-
ney, particularly the slow and patient collection of
enough money to establish and maintain the mission
when Father Ricci and Father Ruggieri got there. The
servants grew impatient with the hospitality they were
compelled to offer to the soldier. It was coming up to the
Chinese Moon Feast, and they came bitterly to the Fathers as time went by, complaining that they had fed this
man far too long, stuffing himself everyday with all the
round white mooncakes he could hold. The soldier grumbled in his turn. He wanted to be back in his own town
for the Moon Feast, for all the family feasting that would
burst upon the country with the crackle of fireworks and
the shouts of happy children, when the gibbous moon
would reach its full. Father Ricci, who was more anxious than any to start the journey, watched the waxing
moon impatiently.

"Tell me about the Moon Feast," he said one hot, exhausting evening to the boy. The Superior had gone out
on the last of his journeys among the merchants to beg
money for the venture, to the house of a Portuguese
called Gaspar Viegas. The others sat and fanned them-

selves in the hot court, and listened to the nightly hum and babble of Macao outside their walls, rising now in a fierce crescendo to the celebrations of the Moon Feast.

The boy beamed and bowed, and tried to slow his rush of talk.

"Honored Father, it is the Moon of the Harvest." He spoke clearly, hands in sleeves and feet side by side, but his lively dark eyes were bright with pleasure that he had something of interest to tell his honored master. "We eat these mooncakes for a long time before the Feast itself, which is on the night that the moon is full. They are very nice, filled full of lotus seeds or chestnut paste." He could not resist a relishing grin, and Father Ricci smiled back agreeably, not saying that he himself had found the mooncakes most unkind to the Italian stomach. "On the night of the Feast itself," the boy went on, "we have big family feasts, and everybody walks out together when night is come, and there is much happiness and rejoicing to see the full moon. The whole night is filled with the banging and the colored stars of the firecrackers that we use to scare the shadows of the devils away from the face of the moon! If we can keep the moon clear, then the devils will stay away from the families for the coming year. The whole family. . . . The whole . . . family . . ."
The light, excited voice dragged suddenly to a stop. "It is all very cheerful and happy," the boy said lamely, but he himself looked neither cheerful now nor happy. Confusion and sadness had filled his face, and his voice faltered and stopped. The dark eyes fixed on the priest

in the yellow lantern light looked lost and wide and desperate with confusion.

"What does the family do?" the priest asked gently.

"I don't know! I don't know!" The boy's thin hands flew up to hide the distress of his face. "How would I know what families do? I who have never had one."

The priest was carefully calm and showed little interest.

"Perhaps," he said indifferently, "you are remembering the feasting in the house of the man who held you as his slave."

Down came the boy's hands. He had recovered, and placed them firmly in his sleeves.

"The Father is good enough to make a joke with me," he said slowly in his precise and beautiful Chinese. "In that House, I did not ever get a mooncake. But there is no sadness for me now, for am I not of the Family of the Lord of Heaven? And his family in this House eat small mooncakes every day, and have all the rice that they want."

It was at this moment that the Superior returned, striding cheerfully around the small circle of the pool.

"So easy," he cried. "I did not even have to ask for it. Gaspar Viegas is a true man of God. It is a sign from Heaven, he says, that this soldier has come to lead Matteo to China, and it is his privilege to provide the money."

Father Ricci did not speak, trying to curb his wild

surge of pure excitement. Now there was no barrier. This time, with God's help, he was truly for China.

Still in silence, he left them, and a little later stood alone in the room they had given him for all his treasures. The wooden cases stood already open on the floor for those things he was going to take; mechanical ambassadors to the great land of China. But there must be something more. Wang P'an knew all about clocks and instruments; that was why he had sent for him. There must be something else he could take as a gift, something truly amazing that would impress this Mandarin at once with the brilliance of the western world. Thoughtfully, he roamed the room, picking up this and that, until absently he came upon a prism of Venetian glass, and held it in his hand, letting the split colors of the lamplight run across the ceiling and up and down the walls. In a moment he knew that he had found what he wanted. There was no glass in China, and this simple fact of reflection, these running colors, would be a wonder new to them, a miracle they had never seen before—a wonder certain to impress. Delighted, he held it up to the light, and the seven colors flashed and wavered over his face.

"May I help the Father put his treasures in the boxes?"

In the open door the boy stood, bowing slightly over his sleeved hands, but his eyes only permitted themselves one astonished flicker at the flying lights, and then came back at once to his master. He had clearly something more on his mind that he would not speak about, his eyes anxious and questioning, ignoring the colors that flowed like water over his face as the priest turned the prism in his fingers.

With a shock, Father Ricci realized what it was that the boy would not ask.

There could be only one thing so important to him that it made him unaware of the device with which he had hoped to amaze a Mandarin. With his mind set on all the millions of souls in China, he had forgotten this one under his feet, and now he did not know what to say to him. The fund for the mission was generous, but who knew how long it would have to last? Was he justified in adding the feeding of yet another mouth?

"The honored Father progresses, but his language is still poor." The boy's voice was desperate, too proud to ask directly.

Still the priest did not answer, and the stilled colors of the prism lay like pools across the floor.

"If I were to come with my master, then who knows but in China I might find my family, and then I would be no further trouble to the Fathers."

Father Ricci thought of the size of the land of China, and the numbers of its immense people, and had not the heart to say that he felt no hope. But hopeless or not, he came to his decision.

"Certainly," he said easily. "You may help to pack my boxes, and you must think too what you may need for yourself, for as you say, my language is poor, and I could not talk in China without you."

There was no noisy rejoicing, only a dignified bend

of the head, betrayed by a wide smile, and the blazing blackness of the bright eyes. Then he caught his manners again and bowed.

"I am glad to go to China," he said, "for I know that I came from there. And while I am very honored to be one of the Family of the Lord of Heaven, my Father will know that this is not a Chinese family."

The priest turned away to hide his smile, and then thought soberly that indeed this was true, but that he himself hoped to take the first steps to change it. When he turned back again, the prism moved in his hand, and now the boy laughed aloud at the flying lights, and did his best to catch them and lift them off the walls, demanding to know the secret of the colored devils.

At last came the dawn that Father Ricci had almost despaired of seeing, when in the gray light of early day the junk for Canton slid out of the harbor and hoisted her brown matting sail to the sluggish air. In the corner of her deck crouched the shapeless figures of two Buddhist priests, their robes the color of the dead dawn light, and their shaven heads deep in the shelter of their hoods. Father Ricci had insisted on this; he and Father Ruggieri must, he said, be recognizable to the Chinese as priests. It could come later to tell them the difference between the bonzes of Buddha and priests of God. Beside them squatted their two servants, Philip silent and inconspicuous in Chinese clothes, and the small, proud figure of the boy, immobile, his face toward China.

They came to Canton in the next dawn, after a night

sliding up the warm turgid waters of the delta through inky darkness sparked with dancing fireflies. On every mud bank the frogs filled the night with their uneasy croaking, harsh against the drumming on the shore as the night watchmen marked the hours past midnight. In the gray light of the new day, on the docks that edged the sprawling city, Father Matteo Ricci set foot at last in China.

"We are staying in the city, my Father?" the boy asked, as he brought them their rice in the tumbledown pavilion that had been offered for their stay in Canton. Father Ricci saw it bleakly as a measure of their welcome.

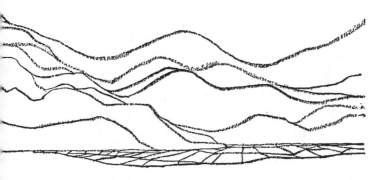

"Not for long," he said. "We are going on to found our mission in Siuching." He nodded at the soldier beyond the door. "The town where he comes from. It is a small town, some days journey inland."

He watched the boy curiously as he spoke, for his usual composure seemed to have left him, and his eyes were wide and puzzled again, as they had been on that night beside the pool.

"You know of Siuching?"

Again the boy shook his head, and his face had a lost look.

"No, my Father," he said. "How would I know of Siuching? I who do not remember China."

Thoughtfully, Father Ricci let him go, and took up his bowl of rice.

There followed days of traveling through soft, cultivated hills, where the small blue figures of the peasants were scattered over the terraced fields and along the hillsides, hoeing their ginger and rice fields, or digging at the honeycomb of ditches that brought water to their land. On all sides there was cultivation and rich growth, and by the time the two Fathers stood on the last hill overlooking Siuching, they were already deeply impressed with the hard work and energy of these toiling, cheerful people. They had spoken to few of them on the way, for those they passed were suspicious of the strange bonzes, with their white skins, and drew to the sides of the sunken roads to let them pass, peering at them shyly from under their mushroom hats of woven straw.

At last the priests stood within sight of the beginning of their mission, and gazed down on the gray, pinkish walls of the small town of Siuching, built snugly in the looping arms of two rivers, in the middle of the tidy, crowded fields that ran up the gentle slopes of the rounded hills.

4

As Father Ricci and Father Ruggieri passed through the town, men sniggered and spat, and drew away from them in the crowded bazaars, strung with their bright waving ribbons. Even though they were wearing the familiar gray robes of the Buddhist, their pale skins and sharp noses betrayed them at once as foreigners. By the time they reached the high walls around the House of Wang P'an, they were followed at a distance by a curious and hostile crowd, who dared come no nearer, and treated them no worse only because of the soldier who escorted them; and because of the might and authority of his master, Governor of the Province.

"You will stay here," Matteo Ricci said to the boy when they had reached the Outer Court. They had been admitted through a small gate beside the huge main gates, which were guarded again on the inside by a vast screen, carved with trees and flowers and whirling dragons, which kept the House of Wang P'an secret from the world, even if his gates should stand wide.

The boy nodded, content to be left. Would it not be with the stumbling words that he himself had taught them, that the Fathers would speak with the Ancient

One of this city? He felt no jealousy of Philip. Philip could go and stand before the Mandarin's table, but his words of low-class Cantonese would be no use at all.

For the first time in his life, standing there in the sun below the writhing dragons, the boy began to fret that he had no name. That small foreign man with the big nose and curls in his hair could say, "I—Philip"—and give his name. He had nothing. Suddenly he minded very much that Philip had a name and he had not. He was tired, and his face fell as he saw the only familiar backs he knew disappearing in the distance through the crimson gates.

The Outer Court of Wang P'an was vast, landscaped like a park, with small curving trees bent to watch their own perfect shapes in clear tiled pools. Paths wandered in careful harmony through small rock gardens, and there were bridges and carved marble archways over the tiled paths, round or shaped like crescent moons. Under trees just bursting into blossom, small marble benches stood here and there for the weary to take their rest.

The boy did not dare to sit down. He did not know what he ought to do, having never before been in a House of such splendor, although the lovely shapes and lines of the garden seemed to fall into some strange familiarity before his eyes. His mind roamed with pleasure over the gardens of the Court.

"Siuching," he said to himself. What did he know of Siuching? Why did he want to whisper it thus? As he told the Father, he had no memory of China.

The Fathers were gone a very long time, and the sun grew higher in the sky. Wearily the boy shifted from one straw-sandaled foot to the other, his feet whispering on the tiles that were growing so hot he could feel it through his thin soles. Somewhere a fountain was playing, the cool tinkle of water falling into a basin. He did not understand where it came from for he had never seen a fountain, but it made him thirsty and he licked his dry lips and leaned wearily against the flaring nostrils of a painted dragon.

Suddenly he was roused by a sound he had not heard before. The massive wooden gates behind the screen were creeping open, groaning on the weight of their hinges and dragged by half a dozen servants. The boy peered back cautiously to see who it was to merit such importance. First came an escort of long-haired ponies, their riders carrying naked swords that glittered in the sun. They trotted away to one side, and the train of servants that followed them with their gongs and trumpets turned away, too, toward their own quarters. That left only a few close attendants and the chair-bearers, who trotted in with a palanquin of such gaudy splendor that the boy gasped. Not the very richest merchant in Macao had come into the streets in anything like this; a mass of finest carving picked with gold and enamel in most brilliant colors. Each of its tasseled poles ended in a carved lotus of such perfection that he felt he could reach out and pick one, and it would have the perfume of a flower. The side curtains were of deepest crimson silk, and the pointed golden roof glittered in the sun as brightly as the swords of the departing guards.

The boy shrank back as it passed around the screen quite close to him; he was more certain than ever that he should not be there. As it reached him, and the servants and the first carriers were past, it was so close that he could have reached out and touched the curtains of crimson silk; and just at that moment, a hoarse voice cried out inside it.

"Wait, bring me the Keeper of the Gate!"

Carefully the carriers set the palanquin on the ground, and a servant ran back to the small pagoda by the main gate. The boy heard the humble salutations of the gatekeeper as he arrived at the other side of the palanquin, bowing before the closed curtains until he presented only the abject top of his round cap. He heard no more, nor could he listen, too sick with fright at where he found himself. He heard nothing, for the thousand mosquitoes of fear buzzling in his brain, and the sweat that trickled down his face had nothing to do with the heat.

The harsh voice rumbled on, interrupted by the anxious one of the gatekeeper, and the boy's almost unseeing eyes were fixed on the crimson curtains immediately opposite him. If the gatekeeper went back exactly as he had come, and the servants moved off quickly, they might not see him. He did not believe it when he first saw the curtains begin to part a fraction, thinking it a trick of his frightened eyes. The voice was still grumbling away on the other side. He watched the crack widen slowly, and his eyes grew until he felt them in his head like saucers, fixed on the widening gap. Suddenly he felt quite cold and calm, waiting for the old, condemning face of some official, who would have him beaten to death before he could even speak. He closed his eyes for a moment, as though that would hide him,

and then he knew it hopeless and opened them again. The curtain was held aside now by a small hand, and he noticed the pearl-like polish on the long fingernails. Then he met the astonished gaze of a girl of about his own age, who stared at him with wide, dark eyes, under startled brows that climbed almost to the shining wings of her black hair. He saw the peach-colored satin of her coat, crusted with gold embroidery on the high collar, and then in that instant she smiled; an immediate, friendly smile, as though she was enchanted to see him there. Then there was a snarl from the hoarse voice on the other side; the crimson curtains snapped shut and there was the unmistakable sound of a slap inside the palanquin. A clear young voice said,

"I am sorry, Eldest Aunt."

Although the boy had cherished his Mandarin tongue, he hardly knew it now that he heard it spoken by a light, easy voice that had obviously never spoken any other. But in a second it was all over. The harsh voice shouted a command, and carriers and servants set off immediately at a jog trot. The Keeper of the Gate moved back the way that he had come, and the boy himself was left leaning on his dragon, holding to its nose and one of its vivid purple claws, with his legs turned to jelly and the sweat of fear drying on his face.

For a moment he wondered if the girl would speak of him, for he knew it to be death to have looked uninvited on the face of any lady of a Chinese noble House. But if she told, he comforted himself, she would have to tell also that she had peered out, and that would make trouble for her too. Besides, there was something friendly and delighted in her smile that made him sure she would not mention the incident.

By the time he saw the familiar shapes of the two Jesuits being bowed out through the inner gate, he was himself again; able to greet them with steady feet together and hidden hands, his head bowed in silent respect, although he longed to ask them how they had fared, and whether they would be allowed to stay in China.

They had fared well. From the moment they were shown into the long Hall of the Mandarin, where he sat in his black robe behind a table draped in crimson damask, they had felt a sympathy in Wang P'an. As they had been instructed, they prostrated themselves on the cool tiles of the floor, foreheads to the ground. But the Mandarin told them to rise, and beckoned them forward, up the long empty room with its few pieces of frail lacquered furniture. When they reached him, they saw with pleasure that the wrinkled ivory face below the wide, winged cap was mild and dignified. The narrow old eyes were shrewd and assessing, but yet warm with welcome.

There was much talking to be done, and never had Father Ricci felt so humble. All his life, he had had the gift of tongues, and now he stood begging in this strange land where he had so much to do, begging in a tongue so difficult that he must only sound ridiculous to those from whom he had so much to ask.

Wang P'an was too courteous to show impatience or amusement, listening with quiet hands and impassive face while Ricci stumbled through the words he knew or looked for help from Philip, to try and tell the reasons for which they had come to China. And yet he dared not give the true reason. Had he said that they had come to convert the Chinese, it would have been death at once. The Chinese believed that they held all the knowledge of the world inside their Flowery Kingdom, and no one from outside dare presume to teach them anything.

They were but poor priests, Father Ricci told the silent Mandarin, who waved his ivory fan gently as he spoke, his eyes on their strange reddened faces. But poor religious who served the Kingdom of Heaven. They asked for nothing except peace, and a small plot of land where they might live, and build a house and a church to worship their own God. They would ask no more and trouble nobody.

Wang P'an gave no answer when the priest stumbled to a halt, but clapped his hands abruptly, and two servants came in carrying fragile colored bowls of fragrant tea. He told them to be seated at a low table in front of him, and with difficulty they squeezed their long European legs into the small space. Had they known more about China, they would have known that although they had had no answer, this was the moment for rejoicing, for the Mandarin would have dismissed them at once if he had been antagonistic to what they asked.

Over the steam of the scented tea, he made polite conversation with them, asking of the strange land to the west from whence they came, and it was clear from his patient, courteous face, that even when he understood them, he did not believe a word of all they said. After the tea bowls were taken away, and hot towels passed to them to wipe their hands and faces, the Chamberlain motioned them to their feet, and they waited for the judgment of Wang P'an, who gave no slightest sign as to what he was about to say. It was the most desperate struggle for the Jesuits to do what was expected of them, and keep their looks as calm and impassive as the Mandarin's own, when he told them that they might settle in Siuching, and that he would grant them land on which to build their house.

With the utmost self-control, they kept quiet and listened. There were conditions. If they were to stay, they must live and dress and speak as Chinese. They must become in all things men of the Middle Kingdom, and be subject to the Emperor of China, the Son of Heaven himself. No more of their kind must come to join them.

Father Ruggieri looked upset, but Father Ricci was calm. He had long ago accepted that he would gain nothing by any other means. This was why he was prostrating himself on the floor before a Chinese Mandarin, in gray Buddhist robes and a shaven head. He bowed to Wang P'an.

"We accept Your Excellency's conditions," he said, "and thank you for your generosity."

Now the faintest flicker of pleasure moved over the ivory face of Wang P'an, but he said no more. The audience was at an end, and the Chamberlain motioned to the priests to follow him to the door.

The boy met them at the gate with the same calm dignity that they were pretending themselves, and they followed the servant to the small pavilion where they might live until they built their own. Only when he was gone and they stood alone in their tiny court with the gate shut did Matteo Ricci turn to his friend with a great cry.

"Michele! We are here and we are here to stay!" He threw out his arms, and Italians again for the blessed moment, he and Father Ruggieri embraced each other in excited gratitude that God had been so good. The boy listened and glowed with pleasure for his beloved Father, so that all uncertainty slipped from his face and his grin was broad and happy.

5

Some days later, in the Women's Courts of the great sprawling pavilions of the House of Wang P'an, the girl who had peered through the curtains stood before her Eldest Aunt, who was the wife of the Mandarin, and in authority over all the women and girls of his Household. Although the girl's attitude was humble and submissive, as became a young girl before the Oldest Woman, her black eyes were bright and rebellious, and when she spoke, her voice was anything but soft and gentle.

"I *want* to go," she said stubbornly. "I want to go, Eldest Aunt. Eldest Uncle has told me all about these foreign bonzes with red faces and big noses and much hair on their hands, which is most peculiar. There is no need for us to go close to them. We could watch them from a distance, and never be seen ourselves."

"There is no need for any woman or girl to go at all," answered Eldest Aunt, and her voice was cold. "It is most improper, like the loud rude tones with which you speak. I do not know what is wrong with you, Youngest Niece, except that your uncle has spoiled you, loving your Father as he did when he was alive. You have become rude and ugly with his kindness, instead of being

53

grateful; but then I think you were too old in many things before you came back to us."

Under the flat, oiled wings of her gray hair, the old woman's contemptuous eyes fell to the girl's feet, and a blush crept up the child's cheeks as warm and pink as her silken coat. This was the most wounding thing that Eldest Aunt could say to her, and the old woman knew it. Much was wrong with Jade in the eyes of the women of the Household, but the worst offense of all was the size and ugliness of her unbound feet. She tried to control her unhappy blush, wishing her rose-colored skirts could reach the ground, but there was a long expanse of white cotton sock before her feet stuck out to shame her, growing larger every day in their neat satin shoes. It was the worst sign of poor breeding that a Chinese woman could show, to have these large and hideous feet, that could run and jump like those of any peasant woman, where a true lady's feet could only totter the few painful steps around the sunlit courts. Constantly she had to remind herself that her quick walking was shocking to the other women, and then slow herself to the awkward pace of their tiny feet.

"It is not my fault," she wanted to cry, as she always did when she was sneered at, knowing exactly what her Eldest Aunt meant when she said she was too old in many things when she had come back to them.

Before she was born, there had been a quarrel, that most unthinkable of all things in a Chinese family. Her father, Wang Jang-fu, had quarreled with his Elder

Brother, Wang P'an, and had fled from the Family House, taking with him his wife and baby son. Wang P'an, loving him dearly, had still been too proud to stop him, thinking only of the honor of his House, and of how Younger Brother was disgracing it. There had been terrible poverty, although the girl did not remember it, and her father, Wang Jang-fu, had died. By the time the repentant Wang P'an had traced them, several years later, there was no longer a young son, only the starving widow and her daughter, whom she called by the pet name of Jade, and who was already two years old; too old to begin the binding of her feet that would have shown good breeding.

Wang P'an had brought them both home, and she had grown up in his House along with her pale, sorrowing shadow of a mother, who closed herself within her own courts, living only to grieve for her husband and son. Wang P'an lavished on the girl Jade all the remorseful love that he should have given to his Younger Brother, and it had pleased him to educate her beyond the usual standard of Chinese girls, because he found her mind quick and lively, and full of curiosity about the wider world outside the Women's Courts.

"Eldest Uncle has spoiled you," the old woman said again severely, her eyes two fierce black slits in the ivory of her face, and from around the cool pavilion that opened on all its sides to the blazing sunshine of the Chinese spring, the other women and girls looked up furtively from their painting and needlework, secretly delighted to hear Wang P'an's favored one scolded. "If you are so unsuitably anxious," the Old One went on, "to see these foreign bonzes, and I understand they are long-faced and peculiar as baboons, then I have no doubt your uncle will allow you, as he allows you everything, to look at them through the lattice secretly, when they come to him for audience."

Jade stuck out a mutinous lower lip, and knew she should not do it. But she was tired of her uncle's walls, shutting her in a cage as gorgeous but just as tight as the golden cage of the colored singing birds in the pavilions. She did not know if she felt like this because of all Wang P'an himself had told her of the world outside his walls, or if it was because she had lived briefly in freedom, even if she did not remember it. She only knew that none of the other girls felt as she did, living happily in their gorgeous cage, never even asking what went on in the streets through which they were carried in their palanquins, curtains sealed against the world. She had a sudden thought of the frightened face of that boy against the screen in the Outer Court, and swallowed back a grin.

"This is different, Eldest Aunt," she pressed on foolishly, "for it is the first time such bonzes have been given leave to stay in China. Eldest Uncle is to mark them out a piece of land and give it to them to build a house and temple. I could peep through my curtains from a distance. No one would see me."

The old woman looked severely at Jade, as if she had not spoken.

"Go to your sleeping room," she said with finality in her hoarse voice. "Go to your sleeping room, and work alone on your needlework until you reach a frame of mind more suitable for a girl. And have care how you walk," she added cruelly.

The floor of yellow tiles seemed as wide as Wang P'an's Outer Court as Jade set out across it, trying to discipline her big feet into tiny steps, and to ignore the ripple of high-pitched giggles that spread across the room as she passed. Cold anger took her before she was halfway across the floor. They were the stupid ones, who could think of nothing but the length of their fingernails and the colors of their bits of silk. Somehow she would see these foreign bonzes for herself. Deliberately she lengthened her stride, and marched through the carved, moon-shaped arch to the sleeping rooms.

The priests had taken several days to choose the site for the building of their first mission, walking with pleasure around the crowded streets of Siuching in the hot sun of spring, the soft air laden with the scent of blossoming trees of a beauty and variety such as they had never seen before. In the end, they chose a spot where the grass ran smooth and sweet down to the loop of the river, with a view across it to the soft brown hills.

"Here," said Matteo Ricci, and looked across the

wide stretch of the blue river, where the fishing cormorants came back to their masters, their throats gorged with young fish. "Here," he said, "we will build the first House of God in China."

Father Ruggieri looked all around him too and nodded in consent, pacing the piece of land with his long legs to measure it, while the boy, standing in apparent quietness beside them, slipped off his straw sandals and wriggled his feet in delight in the cool young grass. There had been no grass in the streets of Macao.

Father Ruggieri came back to where Father Ricci stood, his eyes on the soft curves of the hills, and his staff planted beside him in the soil of his new mission.

"Very good, Matteo," he said. "An excellent choice. But what is that building so close to us? We are getting a lot of attention."

Father Ricci looked at the half-built tower of pale stone that stood at the edge of the meadow by the river. All the workmen had stopped their tasks and were leaning over the walls, watching and talking and laughing at the pale-faced foreigners. The priests did not mind this, having become used in the last few days to being followed everywhere by a curious and usually laughing crowd. They always smiled back, and showed themselves to be as friendly as they could, letting the people follow them wherever they liked. But at the foot of the tower stood a small group of men who were neither friendly nor laughing. They stared at the priests with haughty and unconcealed hostility as they paced their piece of land.

"I wonder who they are," Father Ricci said again, uneasy under the cold stares. "They do not seem to approve of us."

"They are all dressed in the same kind of purple robe," Father Ruggieri observed. "That must mean something. Philip, go to them, and give them our most civil greeting, and tell them we look forward to being friends if they are the owners of the tower."

Philip went as they had told him, and they could see him bowing very respectfully before the group, but that the Chinese appeared to receive his message with disdainful coldness. When he came back he looked crestfallen.

"They are Bachelors, my Father," he said.

"Bachelors?"

"They are Scholars, Father, who have passed all their examinations, but have not yet been given a position in the Government of the country. So they spend their time in reading and in further study under masters. Their chief school is at the Shrine of Confucius, whose philosophy they study."

"Excellent, Philip, excellent!" Father Ricci was delighted. "These are the very sort of people we wish to contact in China. And now we have them as neighbors!" He looked happily toward the tower, where the purple-robed Chinese glared frigidly back.

Philip shook his head.

"They will not make you welcome, my Father," he said. "They are very angry, and very proud. They are

59

most displeased with you, because they are building this tower for themselves for a place of pleasure, and they were going to have this land between it and the river to make a garden, where they might walk under blossom trees and read poetry and contemplate the moon. Now you are planning to build your ugly and unlucky foreign house between them and the river, which will steal all their good luck."

Philip sniggered a little as he repeated all that had been said to him, finding it ridiculous, but Father Ricci did not smile, knowing the great importance of the moon to all educated Chinese, and of good luck to all classes. He was disappointed, but firm. He had no wish to make enemies so soon, but this was the best site that they had seen, and Wang P'an had said that they might have any piece of land they chose. The first Church of God in China was more important than a garden for gazing at the moon; the Bachelors could do that from the top of their tower.

"We will build here," he said firmly. "No doubt they will grow used to us and become friendly."

On the following day the Mandarin himself came in procession through the streets of the town, to make them the formal gift of the land they had chosen. From the river bank they watched him and his train coming down the hill, every common person flying out of the way of his Procession of Might. Lest they might fail to do so, his procession was led by fierce, half-naked guards with long, curling whips, which they cracked and brandished with terrifying cries, frightening off any who might be so hardy as to remain in the path of their exalted master. Behind them came other guards, beating great bronze gongs that drew somber echoes from the brown hills across the river; a troop of soldiers with drawn swords splintering the sunlight, and then a train of servants in the bright livery of their House. Last of all came Wang P'an's Chamberlain, carrying his Seal of Office that must precede him wherever he might travel, and in the middle of it all was Wang P'an himself. He was small and almost insignificant in his black gown, were it not for the frightening immobile dignity with which he sat in his open litter, swaying above the heads of his carriers with his inscrutable ivory face, only his lively eyes shooting all around him, missing nothing. As Jade had found out, Wang P'an's mind was open to the world, even to the world beyond the bounds of China, and in his own territory there was nothing that his sharp, shrewd eyes did not see.

On the grassy space beside the river, starred with the flowers of early summer, the two priests waited and watched the booming, clanging, yelling, whip-cracking procession wind slowly down the deserted hill towards them. Father Ricci was bewildered at the brilliant strangeness of it all, trying to remind himself that all these wild, brightly clad figures were only people like himself, and like all the other people of the western world he came from, small people with souls to strive for. They seemed so arrogantly sure of themselves that the

Jesuit knew a moment of panic-stricken fear that it was he that might be swamped, that far from making them Christians, these swarming people might overwhelm him, and make him Chinese. The procession wound to a halt below the pale stone of the Scholars' tower, and a gathering of men in their purple robes watched the whole ceremony with sour disapproval. Father Ricci shook himself free of his almost superstitious fear and went forward to greet the Mandarin with the deep prostrations of respect that were demanded.

"This is the land you have chosen?"

"This is the land, Excellency."

Standing up ankle-deep in the green, fresh grass, Wang P'an was a small man, but he still held the same dignity, the wide wings of his hat moving a little in the soft wind, and the wild goose symbol of his authority embroidered in heavy silk on the girdle of his robe. Behind him were grouped his courtiers and advisers in their brilliant robes, and their suspicious faces showed that many of them disapproved as much as the Scholars did of giving this land to the foreign bonzes. Wang P'an's own face was calm and unperturbed.

"Have you," he asked, and Father Ricci struggled to understand, rather than get Philip to help him. "Have you, foreigners, thought well over the promises you have made me?" He looked levelly from one to the other and it was clear he meant what he said. "You agree that you will become as the Chinese themselves, if you are allowed to stay."

Father Ricci thought again of his sudden fear that in this great country, this might be exactly what would happen to them, but he pushed the fear aside. Surely his own faith was strong enough for him to become like the Chinese simply to win them to it.

"We have thought," he said steadily. "We have thought, Excellency, and that is how it shall be."

"Then you shall have the land."

Behind him, in the brilliant company, there was a sharp murmur and movement of antagonism, but Wang P'an's face did not flicker. He reached out to his Chamberlain for a Wand of Office, and taking the long, ivory stick in his hand, he set off across the meadow, pacing slowly through the grass in his black satin shoes.

"Here," he said, and laid the wand down in the grass. "From here you may have, until here, and then until here." As he spoke, he walked and drew, until he had made a rectangle in the field with the tip of his wand. Behind him, the two Jesuits looked at each other with crestfallen faces. Dared they object, and ask for more? If they argued now, they might lose all. But the small square of some fifteen feet that the Mandarin had marked would never hold a house and church, however small. But was it better than nothing, they asked each other silently. Would they be wise to hold their tongues?

No, it was not enough. Matteo Ricci breathed a small prayer for help, and bowed deeply before the Mandarin, calling on all the winning good manners for which he had been chosen.

"Excellency," he said, "we are humble strangers from the far lands beyond the bounds of your Emperor's kingdom, and know your generosity in giving us even this much land. But Excellency, this square you mark is enough only for a small dwelling for ourselves and our servants. We have no room to build a temple for the worship of our God."

Now Wang P'an looked at them with interest on his elderly face, the narrow tilted eyes flickering a little.

"We give you permission to worship in the temples of the town of Siuching, like everybody else."

This was being too Chinese, even for Matteo Ricci. There could be no saying of the Holy Mass below the inscrutable smile of a Chinese Buddha. He could only go on and hope not to anger Wang P'an and lose all that he had gained.

"We cannot worship in the temples, Excellency, for we do not worship idols. We worship only the Lord of Heaven himself, for whom there are no idols, and the Lord of Heaven must have a temple of his own."

The Mandarin looked at him thoughtfully for a long time, and the courtiers rumbled and grumbled behind him. Afterwards, Father Ricci said that he thought it was only curiosity that made him give them more land; curiosity to see the building the foreign bonzes would make for their strange god. Whatever prompted him, he moved again after a while and drew another rectangle in the grass beside the first one.

"You may build a temple," he said. "And worship in it whom you please."

The priests did their best to hide their pleasure, such emotion being very bad manners to a well-bred Chinese. Father Ricci simply turned to Father Ruggieri for the presents that they had brought to Wang P'an.

All this the boy had been watching in silence from a respectful distance. At first he was alone, as the people fled from the procession of the Mandarin. Then curiosity began to overcome them, first the builders working on the Scholars' tower, and then the common people who had followed the procession at a distance. In a little while, the boy found himself on the edge of a considerable crowd, which was alive with excitement, yet making no noise lest the guards be angered and turn to drive them away with their long whips.

The boy watched with pride as well as curiosity. Was it not his own master there, speaking directly with the Governor in the slow, careful tones which he had taught him? He drew a deep breath of pleasure and bounced a little on his toes, only to be caught off balance by someone pushing behind him, and almost thrown off his feet.

"Stop pushing, clumsy one," he hissed angrily, for he had been jostled by a boy a little smaller than himself who had thrust too eagerly from behind in his determination to see everything that went on. "Stop pushing! These foreign bonzes are my masters, and I can have you removed if you are a nuisance."

The look of instant fear on the round young face beside him touched him at once with guilt. He remembered all too clearly the recent days when he too had been easily frightened by any fierce threat, having then no Fathers to protect him.

"Do not fear," he added quickly. "I would not do it. They would not let me either," he added in a burst of honesty. "No matter what you did, they would want you here since you are Chinese. They want to be friends with all Chinese, and they could not have too many to watch them."

The other boy did not pay much attention, but the fear left his face, and his eyes rested only on the two gray-robed figures beside the Mandarin.

"Your masters?" he echoed, and the boy nodded importantly.

"They come from the far lands of the West, of which we know nothing," he said. "From the other side of the seas around our Kingdom."

"I know," said the other child, and the boy looked at him curiously. He seemed a bit younger than himself, but his face was round and soft and very clean, with enormous dark eyes and a thick, shining pigtail down to his waist, which was puzzling. Most boys of their age had only just begun to grow the pigtail of manhood. The boy glanced down at his clothes. They were not rich, but very new, the creases still sharp in the folds of the green tunic of heavy cotton, and the white edges of his shoe soles almost unmarked by dust.

"How do you know of the foreigners, Young One?" he demanded a little truculently, and at once the younger boy looked evasive.

"I know only a little," he said quickly, "ignorant that I am. Tell me then of your honorable masters."

The boy was quite willing to take on some of the glory of his Fathers. In a whisper, while Wang P'an and the Jesuits paced out the land, he told the strange, soft-faced boy all about the Mission in Macao, making it twice its size.

"And this Lord of Heaven whom they worship," he concluded grandly, "is the greatest God that has ever been."

"Who is he?"

"Who is who?"

"This Lord of Heaven. Who is he?" Dumbly the boy looked at the innocent face. He had not expected questions and cast desperately round for an answer. Who indeed was this Lord of Heaven? He could find nothing to say, and went on talking, ignoring the question.

"Now my masters have come to Siuching. Siuching," he said again and stopped speaking, as if there was always something about the name that brought him to a halt. "This Mandarin," he went on, indicating Wang P'an with a kindly gesture, "heard of my masters and asked them to come here, knowing of their greatness, and they can do with him what they will. Why are you smiling?"

"I am not. I am not smiling," said the younger boy, and quickly wiped the smile from his lips.

"Tell me of yourself," the boy said then. "You have a family?" He was always curious to hear of other people's families, since he did not have one himself. "What is your name?"

"My name is Chang," the younger boy said, speaking one of the commonest names in China. "And yes, I have a family. I live with my Eldest Uncle and Eldest Aunt. But I do not have a father. My father is dead."

"You have brothers and sisters?" the boy pressed him.

"No, I have none."

Suddenly his round face looked small and withdrawn. There was something about him that made the boy feel protective, and he struggled to find a word of comfort.

At that moment he was relieved to see that something else was happening over on the green meadow. Philip was coming toward the Fathers, bearing the carefully wrapped bundles that held their gifts.

"Look," the boy said hastily to the clouded younger face beside him. "They are giving the Governor the gifts that they have brought him."

"Oh, gifts! Gifts from the lands of the West!"

The boy looked at Chang again. He could not make head or tail of him, so sad one moment and the next so excited that you would think the gifts had been brought for him.

Carefully, Philip unwrapped them and handed them to Father Ricci. First there was a small Italian painting of the Blessed Virgin, which they had brought with them from Rome, and bowing low the priest held it out to the Mandarin.

"This is a picture I have brought Your Excellency. It shows the Mother of the Lord of Heaven. We will be honored if Your Excellency will accept our humble gift."

Wang P'an said nothing, but he blinked rapidly and hesitated a long time before he put out a hand and took the painting. He looked long at the front of it and then turned it over and stared carefully at the back of it. Round and round he turned it several times, and then forgot his immense dignity, handing it on to his courtiers and talking rapidly. Some of them would not touch it at all, and others dropped to the ground to venerate it. All their faces were astonished and a little afraid.

"Philip, can you understand what is the matter?" Father Ricci asked. "It is only a painting."

Philip was struggling with the torrents of excited Mandarin.

"I think," he said, "that they believe it is a real person. Chinese paintings are all flat and in pale colors, and in them people do not look real. They think the Mother of the Lord of Heaven must have strong magic that she can put herself like this into their very hands."

Father Ricci was shocked and amused, but carefully subdued his smile.

"Somehow," he said, "we must make them understand that she cannot, or she will be just an idol to them like the rest."

In his limited Mandarin, he tried to explain to the astonished Wang P'an that this was just a painting, like all those that decorated the walls of his own pavilions, but done in a different way. Wang P'an listened patiently, the picture still turning in his hands, and shook his baffled head.

"The prism, Philip," he said. "Give me the prism now."

The sun was high, and its brilliance split and shivered into blazing color in his hands as he unwrapped the glass, and the flowing lights ran across the grass and over startled feet that jumped away from them. Even the watching crowd could see what was being shown this time, and a long-drawn murmur of amazement ran through it. Father Ricci thought at first that many were going to turn and run away. It was useless to tell them that it was just a piece of glass, for they had never seen glass of any kind, their windows filled with heavy parchment. Later he would explain it all to Wang P'an, who could understand, but for the moment he turned it in his hands and caught the sun in shivering color, running the hot lights across their faces so that they all forgot their dignity and jumped and laughed aloud like children, and felt their hands and faces and their robes to see if the flowing colors had marked them.

It was a little while before Wang P'an would consent to take it in his own hands, but he understood quite quickly once he grasped it that it was meant to catch the sun. Then he stood in the flowering field and the august dignity of his Governorship was forgotten, a happy smile creasing his ivory face as he stood like a child, flickering the broken light over the startled faces of his followers and watching the colors change along the backs of his own hands. Matteo Ricci's simple gift had proved just as strange and overwhelming as he had hoped.

"What is it? What is it?"

Chang pinched the boy in his excitement. There was no longer any need to whisper. The entire crowd was humming with wonder and not a little fear, and Chang's gasping question was lost in all the noise.

The boy rubbed his arm. He himself had long since ceased to be astonished. In the Macao Mission, he had seen such marvels in Father Ricci's workshop that he thought him capable of anything. But he could not find a Chinese word for the prism, for indeed there was no such word in China.

"It is a thing," he said, "to catch the sunlight and hold it inside itself. My master says that all light is made up of these colors, but you can only see them with a thing like this. It is one of the wonders of the world to the west. I myself have seen it and held it in my hand; cold and smooth until the sun takes it."

Beside him, Chang did not take his eyes from the flashing colors.

"I will see it," he said almost to himself, breathless with pleasure.

"How will you see it? My master gives it to the Excellency Wang P'an." The boy glared suspiciously at Chang.

"I see it now," he said. "That is what I meant."

71

In the center of the field, Wang P'an was remembering again to be a Mandarin, gathering himself together and resuming his impassive face, although his delighted

eyes could not leave the prism that still flashed in Ricci's hands. Without one word, he chilled his chattering courtiers into silence.

"We thank you, foreigners," he said formally, "for your wonders that you have shown us from the West. We are much impressed and will be glad to hear more of your foreign knowledge. These wonders I will take home with your permission, to show to the unworthy women of my household."

The priest hastened to tell him that they were gifts that he might keep for himself, but there was no answer nor any change in the Governor's inscrutable face. Father Ricci asked Philip to wrap the gifts up again, and one of Wang P'an's servants was bidden to take them, which he did with obvious fear.

The procession of Wang P'an was forming up again, with the gongs and whips and bells, and the small, immobile figure of dignity at its center. In a very short time, the field by the river was empty again, the procession banging off up the slope as the first shadows crept around the blossoming trees, sparked with the capers of the early fireflies. In the field, in the last moments before the instant dark, the two priests looked at each other, and without speaking turned and walked along the faint lines drawn in the soil by the ivory wand of Wang P'an. The next steps had been taken. The foundations had been marked for the first Church of God in China.

Thick darkness had fallen before the boy in the green suit had passed through the town, and was creeping along the walls of the great House of Wang P'an. He was away from the main gate, where the wall passed through poor streets on the edges of the town, and then ran awhile through the open fields that still lay inside the town walls themselves. The streets were mean and crowded, huddled with small houses of mud and bamboo, so mean that the people had no courts of their own, and ate and slept in the streets outside. Chang picked his way carefully through the shadows, for he knew his green suit was too new and clean for this district, and a knife in the throat would give it quickly to someone who had no suit at all. So he avoided the cooking fires and the acrid torchlight until the wall left the streets altogether, and ran into the dark fields, a small path skirting its base. The carved gate to which he came in the end was no more than a darker shadow in the wall itself, for no lamp hung above it, and there was no sound of life, nor any light inside it. Carefully he peered all around him in the darkness, and then slipped his hand in between the whorls and twists of the carved foliage. Finding the secret spring he looked for, he pressed it, and the whole door slid silently into the thickness of the wall. That part at least was over. He had found this gate when he was a small child, wandering lost and alone in this deserted area of Wang P'an's large estate. The lonely child had held the secret ever since. Leaning back against the gate, Chang tried to steady his breathing and calm his thudding heart for the next stage of the journey. He did not know which part of it he had been most afraid of, but on his way out earlier in the day the mean streets had terrified him, and it had taken all his courage to face them on his way back. The next stretch of the journey was different, but as frightening in a different way.

When he was a little calmer, he set off again. Now he had to walk firmly and openly through the courts, but keeping as much as possible out of the light of the bean oil lamps, and the soft glow of the paper lanterns that hung even from the trees of the Inner Courts. There were many, many boys of his age in the House of Wang P'an, and it was unlikely that anyone would notice him when they had not done so in the high sun this afternoon. This was the quiet time before the evening meal, when the men would sit and talk and smoke a pipe with the women of the House.

It was not difficult. No one paid any attention to the young boy walking firmly through the shadows, and he reached his own sleeping room without being stopped.

Even with the tossing off of the round, buttoned cap, the boy Chang turned back at once into the girl Jade, dressed in a suit that her grieving mother kept hopefully in a pigskin chest against the return of her son.

Jade paused with her white cotton stockings in her hand, and wondered whether Wang P'an would send for her later, as he often did in the evening. Perhaps he would show her the gifts that the foreign bonzes had given him. Her whole bright, pretty face lit up at the thought of holding the strange object that made the colored lights flow around it. Cold, that boy had said; and smooth, until the sun took it.

That boy slave of the bonzes had been a reasonable creature, she thought, pulling on her stockings absently; and handsome too, for a common kind of boy. She would be quite pleased to find him again, and learn more about these foreigners and their Lord of Heaven. As if Eldest Aunt could stop her! She giggled a little with pure excitement. It had been quite safe and easy today; already she had forgotten her fear. Why should she not do it again? And again? She was sick of the inside of Wang P'an's walls, and there was no reason why Chang should not move freely all around Siuching.

6

Later that evening, when all the women were gathered in their own courts after the evening meal, Wang P'an came to them. In the gentle light of the hanging lanterns they were like flowers strewn over the pale tiles of the pavilion floor, sitting on their bolsters in the gleaming gowns of colored silks and satins, vivid with the crusting of embroidery. Their long, delicate hands were busy with needles and fine silks for yet more lovely clothes; or with paint and brushes on small tables, the delicate parchment of fans and screens set out before them. As they worked, two of them sang light, monotonous songs to the tinkling music of small stringed instruments. The fragile voices flowed out the open sides of the pavilion into the court that was sweet and rich with the evening perfume of cherry and magnolia and frangipani, and warm with pools of yellow lantern light above the winding paths and little lakes.

Wang P'an came to them with a warm smile of indulgence on his elderly face. As far as the strictness of Eldest Aunt would allow him, he was gentle and easy toward the many women and girls of his household, keeping his strength and coldness for the outside world.

Now he could think of no greater pleasure to give them all, especially the children, than to show them the flying lights and colors from the small magic stick which the foreign bonzes had given him that afternoon. Before the meal, he had tried to show it to Eldest Aunt, but she would not look at it, saying it was not proper for a Chinese woman to know of things from the outside world. All she needed was in her home, and that was quite enough for any well brought-up woman.

Secretly, he looked forward most of all to seeing the bright interest of his Youngest Niece, whose curiosity about the outside world he encouraged, and whose education he supervised himself, in spite of Eldest Aunt, knowing the child to have a better brain than many of the family sons. This thought he kept very close to himself, for in China it was not believed that a girl could be better than a boy in any way, and Wang P'an would be considered on the edge of madness for having such ideas. But he was a wise and thinking man in all things, with an open mind, which was why the Jesuits were even now about to build their first mission church in his city.

All the women rose as Wang P'an entered their pavilion, tossing the bright silks and paintbrushes aside as they brought their foreheads to the floor in humble prostration.

"Rise, rise," he said. "We are alone, and I have something for you to see."

He had exchanged his black robe of office for one of

cream-colored satin, embroidered with great sprawling dragons in blue and green and scarlet silks with jewels in their eyes. Eldest Aunt made way for him, giving him her chair and standing at his side with downcast eyes as was proper, waiting for him to speak.

He could not wait to show them.

"I have been today, women of my House," he said, "with foreign bonzes who have come from the far world of the West. In exchange for land, they have given me gifts. One of these I think is a woman's toy, being beautiful and a little foolish, even though I do not understand it."

He looked all around them, a ring of downcast eyes under sleek, black hair pinned with bright flowers or jeweled combs, and felt impatient. The strangest treasure he had ever seen, from another world, and they stood as calm and polite as if he told them he had planted a new lotus in the court. Only the bright eyes of Jade could not keep still, flickering up under their dropped lids to his face and to the small wrapped bundles in the hands of his servants behind him.

Wang P'an turned and took the prism from a servant, holding it up to the lantern light so that it glowed and shivered in all its colors, then turned it to send the racing lights across the latticed walls and lozenged windows, up the slender pillars with their crowns like claws, and across the formal, brilliant patterns of the ceiling. There was a moment of stunned silence, and then a sort of chirping gasp of terror. It was Elder Daughter who ran first, staggering away on her tiny feet, her face like lard and squealing with fright. Within seconds all the others followed her, stumbling and chittering, Jade thought contemptuously, like the lovebirds in their great golden cage when one of the cats came and sat on its glittering roof. Only Eldest Aunt stayed at his side, because discipline told her it was her place, but her tortoise face was as pale as the flower of carved ivory in her hair, and her composed hands had left her sleeves to pluck at each other in trembling fear.

"Stupid and unworthy ones," he said. "What is there to harm them? You too, Wife? Better that you go and see that they are not all whipping themselves into fevers. Youngest Niece and I will look at the wonder from the West."

Eldest Aunt shot Jade one furious glance, and she only just managed to bow to her husband before she too scuttled from the pavilion as fast as her tiny feet could carry her.

"Stupid ones," he said again. "Stupid ones. Come close, Youngest Niece, who is not afraid, and see the wonder for yourself."

Jade was across the floor with unseemly speed on her unbound feet, and in the ease that they knew when they were alone, she sat on the floor before her uncle.

"May this stupid and unworthy one hold it in her own hand?" she asked, and could hardly breathe until she got the answer.

Her uncle leaned down and handed it to her, and for several seconds she held it close, feeling the smooth coolness in her hand, exactly as that boy had told her. Then she lifted it to the light, and knew the power and excitement of sending the flowing lights ranging all around the farthest shadows of the pavilion. So rapt was she that she did not think what she was saying, her eyes and mind only on the flying lights.

"See, there is still brilliance, even though there is no sun."

Wang P'an looked at her in sharp astonishment.

"No sun? What do you know of this and the sun?"

Confusion took her and her face crimsoned. She looked at him a long moment with the prism blazing in her hand, and the eyes she looked into were suddenly the sharp, questioning eyes of the Mandarin Wang P'an, and not the mild eyes of her benevolent uncle.

"Honored Uncle," she stammered, and dropped her own eyes. "Honored Uncle, I—I only meant that the sun is the brightest light we know, and so it seems to me that this should be most brilliant with its light."

Wang P'an accepted it, even smiling a small, approving smile. He was always pleased to hear Jade reason things out for herself. He nodded.

"The bonzes showed it to me in the sun today," he said, "and many of my people were frightened, thinking it a devil. But the bigger bonze, Ri-ki, told me that it is only a thing of science, which he will explain to me at another time."

He took it from her, and flashed it again around the room, and the smile of pleasure on his wise, elderly face was as simple as that on her own. Then he showed her the picture, telling her that it looked real since it was painted with a different kind of paint from that which the Chinese used, and that the artist had learned to paint away into the distance, instead of just painting flat. He still could not resist turning it around, to see if he could see anything of the figure's back.

"It is the mother of their Lord of Heaven," he said

then, and they both looked at it in silence, the Mandarin and the child, wondering who in truth this Lord of Heaven might be.

"Now," he said regretfully, "I must give them back."

"Give them back?"

She was so disappointed that she answered him sharply and without politeness, but he did not appear to notice.

"Yes, Youngest," he said, "we must give them back. These foreigners are here by my favor, and it is by my favor that they have their land. If I keep their gifts, it may look as if I have let them stay because of the gifts they have brought me. And no man must be able to point his finger and say that the foreigners have bought Wang P'an."

Jade was silent, thinking of the pure honesty of her uncle, because she knew that he loved the clear stick with the blazing colors just as much as she did. Secretly she thought with excitement of the green suit, and how successfully she had gotten out and back today. It may be she could see the lights again, even if it was not here.

He clapped his hands, and the servants came running to take the gifts and wrap them up again.

Late that night there came a pounding on the door of the small pavilion where the Jesuits lodged. They looked at each other questioningly, and then nodded to Philip, who crossed the tiny court and cautiously opened the green gate. In the lantern light he recognized the badge that he had come to know as that of Wang P'an, embroidered on the coats of the men outside.

"Take us," the older of the two said imperiously, "to your foreign masters."

The Jesuits faced the servants in the dim light of their pavilion, their gray, somber figures dull against the brilliant scarlet of their livery. They were as arrogant and imperious as Wang P'an himself would never be.

"Our master, Excellency Wang P'an." The older spoke again. "Our master, Excellency Wang P'an, bids us bring you these."

Bowing coldly, they placed two bundles on the floor, and were gone as quickly as they came.

"Presents!" Father Ruggieri cried, and Philip and the boy pressed forward to look, for there was but one room in the tiny pavilion. "Presents! He must be well pleased with us, Matteo, to have sent us gifts so soon."

Father Ricci did not answer. There was something unhappily familiar about the shape of the bundles on the floor, even though the wrappings had been changed. Slowly he opened them, and under their disappointed eyes lay the prism and the picture. They looked at them a long time, not speaking, wondering sadly what this might mean.

"Do you think," asked Father Ruggieri in the end, "that we will have to give the land back?"

Matteo Ricci shook his head.

"I don't know. I just do not know what it means. We can only wait and see."

Their faces were long and their hearts heavy as they composed themselves for their night's rest, fearing that almost anything could follow the return of their gifts. The boy watched them, and tried to share the disappointment of his beloved masters, but in his heart he was delighted to have the prism back with them again. There might be a chance to smuggle in that boy in the green suit; Chang, his name was; and show it to him. That would produce a little proper respect in him; he had seemed altogether too superior, although he was younger.

He fell asleep planning happily for this, and slept through his contented night, but through most of it Father Ricci prayed, until the gray and scarlet dawn came creeping over the rounded hills, and struck scent and color from the blossoming trees and the greening rice fields. The day had come for them to begin the building of their mission.

It was to be built in the Western manner, two stories of brick built upon foundations dug into the ground in a fashion unknown to the Chinese, who built their fragile dwellings straight onto the ground, giving them only the support of uprights and pillars, like large, neat boxes.

First the two priests had to count most carefully the limited sum of money which they had brought from Macao, and with it negotiate the purchase of building materials and the hiring of workmen. These men stared and laughed until they were double, for who would begin a building by digging down into the ground? The Jesuits measured and marked the plot, and showed where the foundations must go, and Philip harangued the laughing workmen into their unfamiliar task, until at last the trenches of the new foundations marked the flowering meadow with rifts of fresh, brown earth.

The priests worked as hard as any of the workmen in the strengthening heat of the early summer, but their task was not made easier by the crowds of people who flocked from far and wide to see and laugh at these strange barbarians who looked like Buddhist bonzes, but talked of a strange new Lord of Heaven, and came from some ignorant and unheard-of land far beyond the Great Wall of China. Continually the priests had to stop their work, to show the prism and the picture to chattering crowds who usually came to laugh, and then stayed to marvel, even bowing down in adoration of the flowing, shimmering colors and the picture in which a real person stood.

The boy, whose thin face grew daily rounder and more cheerful, strutted among them full of pride, telling them of the wonders of his masters, and of the magnificent Family of the Lord of Heaven, to which they all belonged.

"And who," the curious Chinese would ask him, "is this Lord of Heaven? Is he to do with the Emperor himself? Is he of the Royal Princes?"

Hastily the boy would change the conversation, more than a little puzzled himself, because if you belonged to a proud Chinese family, the Oldest One was always there in his place as the head of the House, to be seen in all his importance and authority. But even when he and his master Ri-ki struggled to talk of this, the boy could not gather more than that there certainly *was* a Lord of Heaven, who was the Oldest One to all his family, but could not be seen by them. It was too much to understand, but he did his best with the people who questioned him.

"Is not the Oldest Woman the most important person within the private courts of any family," he would ask, "no matter how great her Eldest Son may be?" He would show them then the picture of the Virgin and Child, and puzzled, the people would drift away, saying that the only god these bonzes could show them seemed to be a woman. In all this busy activity for his Fathers, he had forgotten the reason why he had pleaded to come to China. It seemed impossible to think of searching for his family in this teeming mass of people, and for the moment he was busy enough with the affairs of the Family of the Lord of Heaven.

Yet he was delighted one day when he saw again the boy in the green suit, sitting on a heap of newly dug earth, his bright eyes watching the workmen and the two priests. The boy saw Chang with pleasure. He had liked him on the instant, and he had never known a friend, growing tired sometimes of all the grown-up talking of Philip and the Fathers. Eagerly he leaped over a trench and started off across the meadow that was now trodden flat and brown. Then he recalled himself. It was most unsuitable that he should be so eager with this boy Chang, who was no one, and younger than he was himself, when he was the trusted servant of the bonzes who owned the prism, and of the Family of the Lord of Heaven.

Carefully he sauntered around and came up behind Chang, trying to preserve his aloofness; there was something about this younger boy that made him feel he should use his best manners. Chang sat alone, the green cotton knees hunched, and a long stem of flowering grass between his teeth. There was a small, contented smile on his soft, sun-flushed face.

"And have you nothing better to do, Young One," said the boy suddenly from behind him, "than to sit here and watch my masters work? Why are you not at school?"

Chang turned and blinked at him, thinking of the hours of tutors and the sharp questioning in the evenings from Wang P'an. Then he smiled kindly.

"Ah, it is you, insignificant slave of the bonzes," he retorted. "Why are you not there yourself?"

The boy was taken aback. Years of slavery and then life on the streets of Macao had closed his mind to such things as school. He had forgotten it existed for himself.

Quickly he recovered.

"I have no need of school. I am too valuable here to my foreign masters, teaching them all they need to know of the language. It is I who lead them in all their conversations with Excellency Wang P'an the Governor. How else would they be able to speak with him? How else could they have explained to him those treasures which they loaned him?"

He flushed a little, troubled by the broad grin that crept across Chang's face.

"Your masters merely *loaned* Eldest—*loaned* Excellency Wang P'an their treasures?" Chang asked him.

"Truly. For they are more splendid than anything in China, and could not be given lightly to anyone outside the Family of the Lord of Heaven. If you will promise to keep your unworthy hands to yourself, Young One, I will allow you to look at them again some time, now that Excellency the Governor has returned them as he was bidden."

Jade let it all pass and jumped up. It was in the very hope of holding the cool, smooth prism with its shivering color that she had crept out today. She had not minded so much that Eldest Uncle had returned the picture, but she longed for the magical beauty of the prism. Then she remembered that she was Chang, and turned a face of careful indifference toward the boy. Even if she liked him, and she did, she did not have to let him think himself or his possessions too important. He thought himself quite important enough.

"If your masters will allow their youngest slave to show their treasures, I would like to see them now."

Fortunately for the boy and his pride, Father Ricci was endlessly patient, and did not think it too small a matter to try and please any Chinese, in the interest of making them all his friends. He did not mind how young they were, as long as he could hold their interest and talk to them. Smiling, he unwrapped the precious bundles for the thousandth time, looking with pleasure and mild curiosity at the smooth, round face of the child who took the prism so reverently in his fingers. Exactly as the boy had done when he first saw him, this child made an impression of pleasing grace, and had manners of the same beautiful perfection.

Chang sighed as he handed back the prism, bowing over his clasped hands, and beside him the boy beamed in pride and pleasure as complete as if he himself had shaped the smooth planes of glass that caught the colors of the shattered sunlight.

"You are privileged, Young One," the boy said kindly, as they bowed and left Father Ricci, who looked after them with pleasure. It would be good if his boy could find a friend of his own age. It was not enough for a child so young even to be of the Family of the Lord of Heaven. He needed brothers and sisters on earth also.

A small fire of rebellion was building up inside the smooth face of Chang, roused by the feelings of Jade, who was after all the Youngest Niece of the Excellency Governor Wang P'an, in spite of her insignificance in his House. And who was this slave in his blue cotton suit that was too short for him, with his wide eyes and lifted eyebrows, to condescend to her? Heads had rolled in the execution yard of Wang P'an for far less insolence. Yet she had the sense to know that she must be fair. By pretending to be Chang, she had no right to expect any particular respect, and besides, although she would not show it, she liked this boy. But now he had gotten conceited, and she knew how to bring him down. For a moment, sheer terror seized her at what she planned to do. But she must show him.

"Come," she said. "Come with me, and I will show you the treasures of my House."

The boy forgot his dignity.

"Your House?" He laughed derisively. "Ah, Young One," he said, with kindness, "I would not think it would be worth the journey."

The shadows of the sudden dusk were gathering in the meadow, but they did not hide the quick, angry flush on Chang's face.

"It will be worth the journey, slave," he said, and it was Jade who spoke, in the cold voice of Wang P'an.

Obscurely, the boy knew that he had gone too far, even to dishonor the colored scroll or the single bowl of precious jade that his Young One might show him in some humble court. He glanced over at the priests, who were kindling torches to light their work on into the hours of hot darkness. He had never yet left them, unless they had sent him on an errand. A moment he hesitated.

"I will come," he said then, "and pay respect to your treasures."

Chang bowed his head and said nothing, leading the way off immediately up the sloping hill toward the town. As they left, the boy looked back once more across the meadow, now plunged into the instant dark of China, sparked with fireflies and loud with the hoarse croaking of the bull frogs from the river. He noticed that a small procession was setting off from the Scholars' tower toward the working priests, torchlight spattering on their purple robes and their cold, determined faces. He watched for a curious moment, and then turned and followed Chang's fast-moving back into the shadows of the deep tree-lined road.

When they had passed through the busy streets of the bazaars, and were heading into the poorer quarters, the boy nodded to himself resignedly. He had thought this journey would come to little, but if it was in these places that Chang lived, then it would be for even less than that. However, he had come now, and he was prepared to be courteous about it. So that when they threaded their way through the beggars and the cooking fires and the sprawling, dirty children, and Chang drew a little closer to him, he smiled at him in the dim, unhappy light, to show him that he would not look down on him for having nothing to show that would compare with the prism and the picture.

He grew puzzled when they left the last streets, and were in the open fields, threading along the walls of some big estate. Was this boy Chang so very poor that he did not have a home, but only some cave in the country itself? What treasures could he have there, poor boy?

"Chang," he said to the shadow ahead of him in the darkness. Why go farther? "Chang!" To his astonishment, Chang whipped around and clapped a hand across his mouth, gripping his wrist fiercely at the same time.

"Quiet down, slave," he hissed, and the amazed boy fell silent.

In a few more minutes they halted, and with his eyes now used to the dark, the boy could see the outlines of a door, fiercely twined with fine carving, and watched Chang's white blur of a hand creeping through the holes and twists of the design. A soft click and the door slid back, and Chang drew him through it with the same firm grip on his wrist. They were in some sort of meadow. The boy smelled the moist evening smell of grass, and saw the white shapes of pigs penned away to one side, troubling the silent air with their soft grunting. His footsteps quiet and certain, Chang towed him around the edge of the meadow in the shadow of the high wall, until they were in gardens, moving in the darkness of trees, and through faint light over small pools, feeling the steps of bridges under his nervous feet.

By now the proud boy was trembling in cold uncertainty. This seemed no place for either of them to be, but the boy Chang at least knew where he was and where he was going. This seemed like the gardens of some great House, with the lantern lights of the Inner Courts gleaming in the distance ahead. An unknown slave could expect nothing except the cold sharpness of the ax across his neck if he were caught; and lucky too if his death were as merciful even as that.

"Chang!" He tried again, and had difficulty in even finding a whisper to speak his fears. All he got was the firm hand slapped again across his mouth. They were coming up to a large pavilion, the sharp curves of the double roof looped like a darker shadow on the sky, faintly lightened by a rising moon. There was no light where they were, but there was clearly light around on the other side of the pavilion, and the boy decided that before they should reach it, he would turn and run, and escape back into the shadows behind them, although how he would get out of the meadow he did not know.

At that moment Chang pushed him up against the wall of the pavilion, in the deep shadow of one of the veranda pillars.

"On your death," he whispered to him, fiercely, "stay here till I come back."

There was nothing else the boy could do. Chang had vanished into the darkness and he was alone, trembling, and listening to the sound of distant voices and the far, faint lift of music. He gave up his plan to try and run for it; alone he might never even find the carved door, let alone open it. Somewhere quite close he heard a man laugh, suddenly, and he felt the sweat break out all over him as cold as the glass of the prism when he held it in his fingers. By the time Chang came back, he had forgotten all about seeing treasures, or why he was there at all, given over to fear greater than any he had ever known even in the worst moments in the foul back-streets of Macao. There he had seen the justice given out to thieves, and if he were caught, who would believe that he was anything other than a thief who had not yet had the time to steal.

Suddenly like a shadow, Chang was beside him again, and relief was like a blow on the throat.

"It is safe," Chang whispered incomprehensibly. "There are no guests."

The boy did not understand, and tried to say so, but Chang had him again by the wrist and was opening a small door in the pavilion wall. It turned directly onto a flight of stairs running up in the thickness of the wall, softly lit by some lamp that could not be seen. As if he sleepwalked, the boy followed Chang up the tiled steps, noticing the silk-hung walls like a dream, and the gold and enamel post with its writhing dragon at the top of the stairs. They turned then into a long gallery, the walls hung with bright embroidered satin.

"Now." Chang turned to the stupefied boy, and seemed suddenly some inches taller, his soft young face severe and proud.

"There," he said, and lifted a hand to the lattice with

its carefully hidden peepholes. "There, Unworthy One, see the treasures of my House. This is the Women's Gallery," he said, seeing the fear and uncertainty on the face of his unwilling guest. "This is where they come to watch the visitors who are allowed to see the treasures. There is no guard on this side of the pavilion unless there are women in the gallery, for there is no way down. Look, look for yourself at the humble belongings of my House."

Dumbly the boy put his eye to the lattice peephole, stifling a gasp of wonder and sheer terror as he looked down at the floor below. On the level of his amazed eyes, great golden lamps hung from the colored ceiling, throwing their rich, warm light down on all the collected riches of the treasure house of Wang P'an; gleaming on gold and enamel of coffers and caskets; on the brilliant silks and jewels of ceremonial hangings, winking with a fortune in the folds of their embroidery; on the jeweled hafts of sword and scimitar, and the formal headdresses of the ladies of the House. Great bales of furs from the cold North lay against rolls of silk in every color of the summer's flowers, and chests and shelves of finest carving held the pale rich gleam of jade and ivory, alabaster and lapis lazuli. Long the boy stared in utter silence, his eyes coming back ever so often with a sick lurch of fear to the massive figures of the guards who stood along the pale tiles of the floor, the gentle light gleaming on the curve of their swords and the oiled smoothness of their black heads.

Finally he turned, and he and Chang looked at each other in the golden light that flooded through the lattice. The boy took a deep breath and put his hands in his blue sleeves, bowing deeply. It was as well that they needed to whisper, for he had no breath to do more.

"Thank you," he said formally. "Thank you, Young Chang, for doing me the honor to show me these things."

Jade looked at him as he bowed, and like Father Ricci in Macao, she noticed suddenly the light brown hair on his bent head, and for a moment her mind teased her that someone, sometime, had told her something about light brown hair like this. Then she smiled broadly and happily. The honor of Chang was satisfied, and the honor of her House, even if this boy did not know whose it was. Face was saved. She grabbed his hand.

"Quickly," she whispered. "Quickly. I am frightened too. I must get you out."

Good fortune went with them, and they met no one through the deserted gardens to the carved door. At the gate the boy came to a halt, recovering from his stupefaction and his mind beginning to work again.

"Chang," he said urgently, but Chang did not answer, only pushed him through the gate firmly, its click solid and final behind him. He stood there thinking for a long time, feeling the sharp carving of the door bite into his shoulders as he leaned against it, and this made him think inconsequently of the day that Father Ricci had come to Siuching, and he had leaned against the carved screen in the court of Wang P'an and seen the girl grin at him from the palanquin.

"Siuching," he said absently, repeating the word as he always did when it came into his mind, and then he moved away from the gate. But he did not go straight back to the Jesuit pavilion through the streets as he had come. He followed the wall around from the gate, through the fields and through the streets, until even in the gentle moonlight he had no difficulty in recognizing the great gates of the House of Wang P'an, through which he had gone on that first day with his masters. Staring at them, he was more confused and terrified than ever, lifting his hands almost to feel if his head were still safe on his shoulders.

Who was the boy Chang?

And quite apart from his own certain death, what would have happened to his masters and all their plans for China if he and this strange boy had been caught in the pavilions of the Mandarin?

By the time he reached their own pavilion, the Jesuits were too disturbed and anxious themselves even to have noticed his absence. It seemed that the procession of purple robes setting out from the tower as he left with Chang had been a company of Senior Scholars, coming to tell the workmen on the mission site that they must stop all work immediately, as the building had been started on a day of ill omen, and to continue work on it would result in evil consequences for all concerned. The frightened workmen had taken their tools and fled, and now the priests faced the task of building the mission on their own.

7

The Jesuits stood disconsolate above the rising walls of their mission house. The foundations had been dug, and the walls were a few feet high, but now the site was empty, the workmen fled before the threats of the Scholars. Nor was there any promise of when they would come back. They would not touch their tools again until the Professor of the Scholars had calculated a more suitable day from the Calendar of Omens, so that their fresh start could bring no more ill luck.

"And the Professor," said Father Ricci dolefully, "will make that task take as long as possible. They are very angry about losing their blossoming garden for gazing at the moon. Especially to foreigners like us."

"My Fathers." The boy bowed beside them.

"Yes?" Father Ricci looked at him a moment and noticed that he seemed almost as tired and anxious as they were themselves. The priest was touched at his concern for the mission.

"What is it, Boy?" he asked kindly.

The boy was indeed anxious, but not entirely for the progress of the mission. For all his talk about belonging to the Family of the Lord of Heaven, he was Chinese enough to believe in all portents and ill omens, and his conscience plagued him that last night he might have committed an offense so dreadful as to bring ill luck to the House of the Fathers which he served.

"Honored Fathers," he said diffidently, "it is not only that the Scholars think you have begun to build on a day of ill omen. It is also shown by the stars that the place in which you have begun to build your house throws a shadow of ill luck on their tower."

"Where have you heard this?"

"My Fathers, it is the talk of the bazaars." How could he say that he had heard it from the boy Chang, who had entry to the House of Wang P'an? At the very memory of last night, he grew pale and sweat beaded his forehead. Father Ricci knew fresh pleasure in the boy's interest in the mission and all that concerned it.

"Do not trouble yourself, Boy," he said. "The Lord of Heaven protects all his family, even the most humble, against such things as charms and omens, so that we do not need to notice them."

That is good, thought the boy, but would he protect me against the fury of Wang P'an if he found me within his gates, and inside his very Court of Treasures?

"Come, Michele," Father Ricci said determinedly. "We will have to build it all ourselves."

"All of it? Alone?" Father Ruggieri was not unwilling, and had worked strongly beside the Chinese workmen, but he knew that both of them were unused to the growing heat of the Chinese summer. The task was too big.

Matteo Ricci was unperturbed.

"We cannot have these people thinking that we are swayed by their omens and threats. We must go on, Michele, if only to show them that our God is above such things."

So alone they toiled through the long, hot days, when the river shrank away from its banks, and the frogs on the mudbanks filled the night with their harsh croaking. The boy worked beside them eagerly. It was partly due to his love for them, and largely to his fear of stirring one step away from them until he was sure no vengeance was going to fall on him from the House of Wang P'an. The sweat grew cold on his forehead as he thought how he and Chang may well have been watched, thinking themselves alone. Stripped to the waist in the steaming heat, he bent his face over his work and made himself as inconspicuous as possible.

Once more the Chinese crowds, smaller now, came flocking to see them work, hoping to be present at the catastrophe which must surely overtake these mad foreigners who dared to ignore the days of ill omen, and the proud, terrifying authority of the Scholars.

Every day the boy looked closely at all the people who came to stare, hoping to see the green suit and to confront young Chang and demand of him who or what he was in the House of Wang P'an. But the days passed and Chang did not appear, and a new fear began to settle on the boy. It may be that after he had gotten away, Chang had been caught in the Inner Courts where he had no right to be, and had been put to death. In such a great House this could happen to a lesser servant, and he began to grieve that it was his conceit about the prism that had driven Chang to what he did. Round and round his thoughts went, with the stick that stirred the mud for binding bricks, and he recalled the soft, cheerful face of Chang, and could have wept that he may have brought him to the headsman's sword. Several times he put down his stick and looked at the strong, level face of Father Ricci and was determined to tell him the whole story. But he could not. He did not understand much about this Lord of Heaven, or why it was so very important his family should come to China, but he knew that it *was* important to Ri-ki, who had taken him starving from the streets of Macao and given him all the things he had never had. Well, perhaps not a name yet, but a family and a home.

"My family," he said to himself proudly. "My family is of the Lord of Heaven, and my home is Siuching." Siuching. No, he could not tell Ri-ki. Even to know would be a danger for him, and nothing must be done, *nothing*, to harm his plan to stay forever in China.

The boy's face grew thin again, and so did those of the priests, toiling away in the moist, exhausting heat. Within a short time they were utterly defeated by the heavy work, and it was clear that the task was too much for them.

"It is no use, Michele," Father Ricci said in the end. The steamy night heat filled their tiny pavilion, almost sickeningly heavy with the perfume of lilies and carnations from the court, and thick with the flittering brilliance of the fireflies against the small glow of their bean oil lamps. He looked at the broken blisters and lacerated skin of his hands, and knew the other priest's were no better. He felt the weakness that prostrated him from working in this climate, and knew Michele's was as great as his own.

"It is no use," he said again. "The Scholars will be proved right if we go on as we are, because we will simply die before we ever build our house, and what omen for God could be more evil than that? I will go to Wang P'an and plead to get our workmen back, or at least hurry them in choosing a day to begin again."

He felt depressed and close to defeat, baffled by the rigid Chinese mind that was so bound by rules and charms and omens. He found it almost impossible to break these down since the Chinese language did not even have words for the different Christian ideas that he would wish to teach. But the work must go on. He wiped the sweat of the cloying night from his forehead.

"I will go to Wang P'an."

On Father Ruggieri's forehead the sweat was as much from relief as from the heat. He would have carried on until he died beside his Superior, but he was a heavier man than Father Ricci, and felt the heat even more.

"You are right, Matteo," he said as mildly as he could, "but how will you speak with him? Remember Philip went yesterday to Canton in the hope of money from

Macao. Have you enough Mandarin to speak alone with Wang P'an?"

"I will take the boy. His speech will be a credit to us, and Philip is not here to be offended."

Michele nodded. The boy was a far better interpreter where people like the Mandarin were concerned, putting their answers into simple words which the priests could understand.

The boy showed none of the pride that Matteo Ricci had expected when he told him the next morning that he was taking him to the House of the Governor. His face grew white as the waxy camellias behind his head, and his dark eyes wide as pools.

"The House of Wang P'an!" he whispered. "I cannot go there." He spoke the words before he could stop them, but the priest took his objection for simple nervousness.

"It is nothing," he said. "Nothing at all. Wang P'an is a most kindly man, though fierce enough, I dare say, with those who have done wrong. But we are going to him only for his help, so we have nothing to fear."

Dumbly the boy stared at him.

"I need you," Father Ricci said. "I cannot speak well enough yet for myself, and Philip is away. I need you."

There was nothing more to be said. His Father, who had given him his life, needed him, and he must do whatever he was asked.

"You will be clean," Father Ricci went on, "and do me credit."

The boy nodded and bowed, the strange light hair bleached even lighter by the sun. Carefully he did as the Father had asked him, bathing in the shallows of the river, but with no eyes for the fading green hills rounding beyond the bright water, or the swooping shadows of the fishing cormorants. His mind was too full of fear, but the fear was sparked with the strong hope that too many days had passed now for him to be in any danger, even inside the House of Wang P'an. If they had seen him, they would have come for him by now.

There was something else on his mind too. When he was cleaned and dressed in a fresh suit of blue cotton, he came slowly to Father Ruggieri, bowing before him with an agony of shyness on his young face.

"Mi-kli," he said, hesitantly, "I am going with the Father Ri-ki to the great House of Wang P'an."

Michele looked over his book.

"Yes. You are very privileged."

The boy's manners were too good for him to move even his toes, but his whole body was tense with what he was trying to say.

"Mi-kli," he said desperately, "I do not want to disgrace the Fathers with my unworthy appearance in the House of the Governor."

The Jesuit looked at him and wondered where it was all leading. The boy was spotlessly clean and dignified, and he thought to himself that Matteo had been right in seeing some special quality in this boy. He would disgrace no one, and the priest said as much to him, but the look of anguish on the boy's face grew no less.

"I am almost thirteen," he blurted out. "I know by my birth chain. Almost thirteen and my hair hangs loose like a child, and I have no cash to give a barber to make me a pigtail, nor have we any women in the house to do it for me. It should be the pride of my mother at this age to make me a pigtail that I might show myself a man, but the women of the Lord of Heaven are not with us."

The priest understood but was careful not to smile. He turned to a small pigskin coffer where they kept their meager store of cash, and gave the boy a handful of the small, square coins, threaded on a string.

"As you say," he said carefully, "we have no women in this house, and Ri-ki and I have been thoughtless not to understand that you are now a man. Why did you ask me," he added curiously, "and not Ri-ki?"

The fleeting expression on the boy's face had nothing to do with manliness; it was of pure, childish pleasure.

"I did not wish him to see me," he said, "until it was done."

Later, when they were ready to set out for the House of Wang P'an, he was very calm and severe looking, the flat, handsome planes of his face made clearer by the scraped back hair. The little oiled pigtail that stuck out at the back was barely long enough to show below the brim of his straw hat, and his proud face defied any comment.

Father Ricci, like his brother priest, was careful to make none.

They walked one behind the other through the crowded town, the foreign bonze and the Chinese boy, with all the dignity of Wang P'an himself, but by the time they reached the huge green gates with their curling dragons the boy had forgotten dignity and was shaking in his straw sandals like bamboo leaves in a storm. The gate-keeper admitted them, and he bent his head in seeming humility, hiding his face with the wide brim of his hat. There was the usual long delay of patient waiting in the Outer Court, and the boy slowly gained courage as no one came near them, and began to look about him, trying to recognize anything he had seen on that terrifying night.

There was constant traffic of people moving through the wide avenues to audiences with the Governor; poor people in humble cotton clothes and richly dressed officials preceded by their gongs and servants; there were palanquins with close-drawn curtains, and once a gaggle of wretched prisoners, dragged along by their guards with ropes around their necks, and their hands fettered in heavy wooden frames. The boy looked at them and knew a coldness around his neck, but he saw no sign of a gold-roofed palanquin with crimson curtains, or of a boy in a green suit. Odd, he thought, that he should know of two people in this great House, and yet have no idea who either of them were. They could not have anything to do with each other. The boy Chang was clearly a ser-

vant of some kind, while the girl with the smile was an important lady.

So he brooded and watched through the bright passing of the day, and the Jesuit in his gray robes squatted humbly beside him on the tiles of the court, and brooded too, thinking of his mission and begging God to intercede for him with Wang P'an. It was afternoon when at last the servant of the Chamberlain came out and called the name of Ri-ki, and they went in to their audience with Wang P'an.

The priest was granted a little more favor now, and the Mandarin did not receive him in his vast Pavilion of Audience, but in a smaller room, opening off a tiny court that held no more than one exquisite pine tree, bent above a pool lined with scarlet tiles. Wang P'an was smiling, and received them kindly, bidding them raise themselves from the floor, and looking with amused tolerance at the size and age of Father Ricci's interpreter. His expression changed as the boy laid out the claims of the Jesuits against the Scholars in his clear Chinese, and he watched him carefully as he spoke. It was beneath him to address such a person directly, but he turned to the priest.

"Who is your servant?" he asked, and knowing his place, the boy stood with downcast eyes as though he were not there.

"I took him, Excellency, off the streets of Macao, where he starved, when I had heard him speak."

"Where did he learn such speech?"

111

Father Ricci shook his head and wished that they could come to the point of the audience, but he held his peace, knowing that such directness was not the way of China. He had stated his case, and now everything of interest to Wang P'an would be talked of before any decision was made.

"I do not know, Excellency." The boy answered for him, as if he did not speak of himself. "He says he has always spoken thus."

Wang P'an looked at the boy with his quiet, expressionless eyes, and the sun moved around the fretted carving of the roof, throwing a bright pattern of light across the tiled floor, and falling on the boy's newly smoothed head so that it looked almost fair. Father Ricci was startled to see Wang P'an for one brief moment shaken from his rigid composure; his wise, calm face crinkled with some obvious pain as he stared at the boy. The priest could see no reason for his distress, and almost at once the Governor settled back into his chair, his expression calm again, and clapped his hands for the servants to bring the ceremonial tea without which the interview could not be concluded.

"I observe," the Mandarin said almost to himself, "the strange color of your servant's hair. I have seen such hair but once before."

The priest knew better than to presume any question, and settled himself respectfully to the patient ceremony of drinking tea, and to try and tell Wang P'an in the strange, difficult language of some of the wisdom and curiosities of the Western world.

The boy moved back to stand motionless against the wall of fretted carving. Hands in his sleeves, he stood to wait until his master needed him again, pleasing himself by the tiniest motions of his head that allowed him to feel the small stump of the proud, precious pigtail rubbing against the carving at his back.

Suddenly he felt his pigtail jerked, painfully, catching all the short, newly plaited hairs at the nape of his neck. Tears ran into his eyes in his attempts to keep silent, and his anguished eyes flew around to Wang P'an and his servants, to see if anyone had heard the small grunt he had failed to keep back. Truly death walked at his shoulder in this house! To have cried aloud for no reason in the presence of the Mandarin! No Lord of Heaven could have saved him!

He breathed deeply and got control of himself, looking sideways under downcast lids to try and see what was happening behind him. There must be someone behind the lattice, able to see without being seen, exactly as he and Chang had looked at Wang P'an's treasures that other night. Again his pigtail was pulled, more gently this time, and the softest whisper spoke from behind the carving.

"Aieee! It is a pigtail. The youngest slave is a man!"

Frantically he slid his eyes around.

"Be gone!" he hissed desperately between his teeth. This boy Chang was looking for his death! Who was he that he crept like this through the House of Wang P'an, knowing all its secrets? Another soft jerk, and the sweat that broke out all over him had nothing to do with the patterned sun that flooded the floor.

"Such a *small* pigtail!" The light, soft whisper teased him. "I am younger than you are, and I have a pigtail to my waist."

This did not help to calm him. One of the chief reasons that he had begged cash to visit the barber was the thought that he might see young Chang, and would be shamed once more by the sight of the rich, black pigtail down to his waist.

"Poor bonzes." The soft teasing voice went on. "They cannot build a house for their treasures because the silly, pompous Scholars will not let them. Poor bonzes."

How did Chang know about the Scholars? He had never been near the site by the river again. Curiosity almost overcame the boy's fear for a moment, and he stopped himself with difficulty from whipping around to the lattice to ask all the questions he wanted. This maddening boy was everywhere and knew everything. But he thought of the cold edge of a sword along his neck, and fear took him again, keeping his glistening face to the front and his downcast eyes on the floor. Fortunately at that moment, the servants came in with the hot, steaming towels for the Mandarin and his guest to wipe their faces and hands. With ritual bowing and respect, the tea drinking was over.

Now the opinion of Wang P'an would be given, and

since the talk was of China, and not of the strange world to the west, the boy could step forward into safety, to be of use again.

The Mandarin gave his judgment. He would not wish, he said, to overrule the Scholars by blunt use of authority. They were very important people with much power, who would one day be governors exactly as himself. But he suggested that Ri-ki should go to their school at the Shrine of Confucius and talk there with the Mandarin who was in authority over them. He was to tell him that he, Wang P'an, had permitted these bonzes to be in Siuching, and to ask him to make some agreeable arrangement. With this smooth and courteous suggestion the Jesuit had to be content, praying that he might find the Professor of Scholars as wise and reasonable as Wang P'an himself.

The boy could not wait to get away. No dignified progress was fast enough for him to get out of the House of Wang P'an, but he was forced to walk at the pace of his master, who was compelled in turn to walk at the slow, pompous pace of the Chamberlain who led him from the Inner Courts; who in turn handed him on to the slow pace of the Keeper of the Outer Courts; who then handed him on to the Keeper of the Gate, who was a very old man and whose pace was the slowest of all. There was plenty of time for him to flick his apparently humble eyes around him for a sight of Chang, but he saw nothing of him. The only thing that startled him was a quick spurt of laughter from behind a screen as they waited to be let out the Lotus gate from the private courts. He saw by the angry frown of the Chamberlain that he had heard it too, but it could not have been Chang because it was quite certainly a girl's laughter.

The Professor of Scholars was much more proud and arrogant than the quiet, wise Wang P'an. Several days later he received the priest and the boy in the Golden Shrine of the Sage Confucius, Father of All Knowledge, seated in his carved chair in the flowing purple robes of his Scholarship. His small, sharp beard pointed at them in derision and he clearly showed his contempt for the ignorant barbarian who had to bring a child to speak for him. But he dared not go against Wang P'an, and was compelled to admit that the foreign bonzes had permission to be in Siuching and also to build.

Reluctantly, he made a compromise. The foreigners should leave their site for the purpose for which the Scholars had planned it—a garden for their peacock parading, reciting poems, and dropping gems of wisdom and staring at the moon. They would give another site for the house and temple of the foreign bonzes, and in addition some building materials from the tower, to make up for what had been wasted. There was nothing to do but agree, and with much bowing and cold respect, Matteo Ricci left the Shrine of Confucius, and faced for the second time the building of the first church in China.

Father Ruggieri thought then that all their troubles were over, and chided Father Ricci that evening for his long face and his refusal to rejoice with him.

116

"What is wrong now?" he cried. "Is everything not set for us now?"

"Ah, Michele," Father Ricci answered, and his face was still drawn with anxiety. "It is not as simple as that."

"Why?"

"The old story." Father Ricci spread his hands. "We have no money left, Michele. None."

"None?"

"I have had no word from Philip in Canton. If anything had come he would be back by now. The materials they will give us from the tower will do more than start us. Somewhere we must get money."

"Wang P'an?"

Father Ruggieri was as doubtful as his voice, and Father Ricci crushed the idea at once.

"Impossible. He has done more than we ever dared to hope for in giving us his protection. How could we ask money from him for the conversion of his people? Although, Michele, before God I begin to wonder how we ever will convert them. Even when we speak the language fluently, there is no word in it for God. How do we begin?"

Father Ruggieri urged him from his mood of depression.

"We begin as you have always said, Matteo. By example. And the first example we must offer them is a church. So we must raise some money."

"Granted. But how?"

"Let us pawn the prism."

"The prism!" Father Ricci stared at him. "Pawn it!"

"Pawn it." Michele was quite firm. "We must be practical. Have you not noticed that half the shops in the bazaars are those of moneylenders? It is the biggest Chinese business. We will get plenty for our magic prism."

"In faith, Michele, you are right. Why not? It is strange to pawn the very gift I chose so carefully for the Governor of Siuching, but this will be serving the ways of God just as well."

He took the boy with him the next day, and they threaded their way through the crowded, noisy streets, walking always in a little space of silence left for the strange foreigners. The people had come to understand that although the priests appeared to be Buddhists, they were in truth only dressed like that, and were really something far more fearsome. So they never had to push through the crowds, a space of suspicion opening always before them.

In the hot, curtained booth of the first moneylender, a wizened old man crouched blinking his wrinkled eyelids in the light of his tiny lamp. At the sight of his small light shattered in the prism, his ancient eyes rolled with fright, and he began to shriek and gibber, throwing himself about in paroxysms of terror and screaming at them to go away. Hastily, the Jesuit thrust it into the folds of his robes, and they pushed hastily out of the booth in the face of a gathering crowd. Behind them, the old man continued to shriek and moan.

"In truth," gasped Father Ricci as they got out, the boy

doubled up with laughter. "In truth, but we must find a younger one, lest we frighten him to death!"

He spoke in Italian first, and then in Chinese to the boy, and they were both grinning in helpless amusement as they peered carefully into the other booths. There was plenty of choice, and they had not much trouble in finding a young moneylender, who had already seen the prism when it was shown to the Mandarin down by the river. He was indeed delighted to have it in his possession for a while, feeling it would bring him much honor among his friends. He was a hard-faced man with cold eyes, and watching the priest, he sensed his desperate need, and so gave him only half the money he needed, hoping even then that the prism might be his for good.

8

The moist days of summer drifted into dry heat, when the grass browned on the hills beyond the river, and the cormorants dived in the shrinking water for fish that were already dead. Before almost every door in the town, a small, pot-bellied idol was put out in the full heat of the exhausting sun. On his way through the streets, the boy looked at these and then with increasing anxiety at the empty door of the mission house, that was now rising to its roof.

"Ri-ki, my Father," he said doubtfully, for he knew that this business of gods was not the same in the House of the Lord of Heaven as it was in China. "My Father, should we not have a rain god, like everybody else?"

Father Ricci looked at him, his mind still half on the clock he was assembling on the table of the roofless living room. Wang P'an came often to the new site, and was deeply interested in all the mechanical devices the priest had to show him. His interest must be held, and Father Ricci worked to see that there was always something new to show him. Now he took the magnifying glass from his eye and laid down the tiny wheels.

"Why should we have a rain god?"

Early on he had learned how useless it was to say to a Chinese directly that this or that was wrong, and that the Christian faith taught otherwise. First they must be allowed to make clear what they thought themselves; then led through that to the Christian idea. No Chinese would listen at once to foreign ideas. This he practiced even with the boy, who was intelligent and close beside them at all times, yet no nearer to understanding Christianity than when they had first found him in Macao. With cheerful willingness he did everything they said, and assured them gaily that he believed all they told him, but he obviously understood nothing.

"When it is hot, my Father, like this, and does not rain, so that the crops wither and the people begin to go hungry, they all take their rain gods and put them in the sun, so that they can feel how hot and unpleasant it is, and do their job of bringing rain. How can the rain god know the need for rain if he is kept in a cool house, and does not feel the heat? And I am afraid, Ri-ki, that if we do not have a rain god, when the rain does come, it may avoid us down here by the river, and pour only on the hills. It has been known to happen."

"And were we here when it happened?" The priest smiled at the boy, who shook his head.

"Then," said Father Ricci reasonably, "it had nothing to do with the rain god that we do not have." The boy gave a shamefaced grin.

Patiently the priest put aside his tools. No Chinese was too unimportant to be led even a small way from his false gods. And the boy was intelligent and talkative; he would tell others.

With great care, in his limited words, the priest told him how all the weather was in the hands of the Lord of Heaven, as were all the workings of the wonderful world which He had made. He explained as best he could how the rain had nothing to do with any idol, but with the way that clouds gathered over the hills, and because of the high land, were more likely to fall as rain there than in the valley of the river.

The boy's face was polite and wide-eyed, and he made no comment when the priest had finished, bowing deeply and thanking him for the information. Looking out afterward from the uncovered window, Father Ricci saw him standing staring at the hills with an expression of acute puzzlement and dismay on his round face, and when the priest went out later on, there was a Chinese good luck sign in fresh paint on the lintel of the door. He sighed. This, he supposed, was as much as he could hope for for a long time; that the Chinese would listen with the utmost politeness, and then do exactly as they had done before. It was only, he knew, the fact that the boy had no cash to buy one, that stopped them having a pot-bellied idol outside their own door, seeking the rain that God would send in His own good time.

By the time of the Festival of the Coming of the Frost, the Jesuit mission building in Siuching was finished, a mere two rooms of humble size, one in which they lived and slept, and the other for the first Christian church in China.

It was very simple, and very sparse in its furnishings, but the two priests could not thank God sufficiently for allowing them to progress so far. The boy was bursting with pride and importance, for now he not only had a family, but a house as well. Two houses indeed, for one-half of this strange pavilion was the House of the Foreign Bonzes, and the other half the House of the Lord of Heaven. And he belonged to both of them. The only shadow on his young face now that he had a home, a family, and the pigtail of a man, was that he still had no name.

Understanding and respect had grown between Matteo Ricci and the calm, strong, incorruptible Wang P'an. When he got news that the building was at last completed, the gongs and cymbals and cracking whips of his procession could soon be heard approaching through the dusty streets, and the Jesuits and the boy prostrated themselves at the doorway of their new church. As the Mandarin and the priests passed inside, the boy's eyes skimmed hopefully over the vast retinue, but there was no boy in a green suit.

Inside, Wang P'an walked gravely through the tiny church, looking carefully at the altar with its small red lamps, and the rosary beads hanging beside it, and the holy pictures on the walls. At the door, he turned and looked back at it all, his ivory face blanched by the shadows, and very thoughtful.

"I have struggled much to understand you, Ri-ki," he said, "and the talk you have made with me of the One True God whom you worship, and that he is Lord of Heaven and Earth. But now that I have seen your temple, I know that you are only Buddhists."

The two priests almost groaned aloud, but carefully did not look at each other, holding to the same calm dignity as the Mandarin himself.

"Excellency," said Matteo Ricci, and begged God to help him with the words, "most humbly your servants ask permission to contradict you. We are not Buddhists. We dress as they do to avoid upsetting your people by our strange clothes and looks, but we are priests of the One True Christian God, who is not Buddha."

Wang P'an looked around again, and then one thin pale hand came out of his black sleeve to point an ivory fan at the lamps and the altar and the beads and holy pictures.

"These things, Ri-ki," he said, "are the things of Buddha. It may be that you are different Buddhists, for there are many kinds. But you are priests of Buddha."

Helpless, they kept their eyes to the ground and did not argue, knowing from all they had seen in the temples that what he said was true, and that in all things they looked like Buddhists. How to argue with a despot of a culture so old and rigid that it barely allowed the existence of a world outside its walls? And they must never anger Wang P'an. Let him for the moment think them sons of Buddha. Wang P'an, however, was a wise man, and a Mandarin, brought up in the strictest rules of good manners and behavior. He had sensed the dismay of the bonzes at what he had said, so he searched for the polite and careful word that would bridge the disagreement and leave everybody satisfied. His eyes fell on the beautiful painting of the Virgin and Child, which the Jesuits had hung above their altar.

"There is one thing," said Wang P'an then with infinite courtesy. "I know of no other Buddhists whose god is a woman. In that you are different; that your god is a woman."

This time there was no danger of the two priests arguing with him, for they stood speechless, looking from each other to the painting of Our Lady. Nor did Wang P'an notice their distress this time, for he had already turned out of the door of the temple, as he called it, much more anxious to see the Jesuit work which interested him most; the collection of clocks and instruments with which Father Ricci occupied most of the space in their tiny living room.

When at last he left, well satisfied with all he had seen of these revolving, ticking marvels, he stood before the door of the mission and held out a hand to a servant, who laid in it a large, decorated scroll.

"Ri-ki," he said, looking up at the tall Jesuit, who always tried to appear small in his presence, so that he might not offend with his great height and size. "Ri-ki, it pleases me, Wang P'an, that you have come to settle in my town, and it may be that we can learn much from

each other. But I know that my Scholars, who are set in their ways and their teaching, do not make you welcome, and would like to turn my people against you. So I, who am Father and Mother of them all, give you this scroll to protect you and to protect your House. Hang it outside your door and it will tell all who come that you are here with my consent, and none may molest you. I also give you a scroll to keep in your chest, saying that I have given you this land, and that I will also give you protection on any journeys you make from here to Macao."

Their prostrations in the dust of his departure were more now than mere correct behavior. There was nothing more important than this deed to the land and the scroll of safety for their doorpost, for a Chinese would find his way around anything that was said to him, but the written word was absolute.

As he scrambled to his feet when Wang P'an was past, the boy carefully scanned the procession once more. He could not really believe that Chang was dead, and yet he must be a close servant who had such freedom of his master's house. Then why was he not in attendance on the Mandarin today? Irritably he kicked a stone. What was the use of the scroll of safety and their new house and temple and all their grandeur, if there was no one to whom he could boast about it?

Beyond him the two Jesuits embraced each other, to the disgust and amusement of the Chinese about them. Such a display of emotion was in the worst taste and manners. But for once even Matteo Ricci was not concerned with the Chinese.

"Our Church is built, Michele!" he said over and over again. "Our Church is built!" He looked down at the beautifully written scroll in his hands. "And this will keep it safe. We need fret no more that it will stay here. God is very good, Michele." Then he added ruefully, "But we must do something about the idea that He is a woman!"

They laughed together for one precious, lighthearted moment, and then Father Ricci's face grew grave again.

"I must be careful," he sighed. "Perhaps I am rejoicing too soon. Our Church is built, and Wang P'an has guaranteed its safety, but unless Philip comes back from Canton with money, we are again in trouble."

They could do no more than wait for Philip, who finally came back from Canton when all the dried brush had been cut from the hillsides, and piled around the houses against the first frosts that blanched the red earth of the terraced fields. He came with a long face and a nose nipped red by the cold of his tedious journey, rubbing his hands before their small stove and bursting out his tale of disappointment.

"There is nothing, my masters," he said. "Nothing. Not so much as one silver tael. I have waited weeks, as you see, in Canton, and met junk after junk, but there was nothing on them for us. Nothing but messages of storm and shipwreck and disaster, and of weeping people waiting in Macao for their friends who are lost on ships that will never come. There is nothing, my Fathers," he said again.

In silence they looked at each other, and the boy watched them from the corner of the small room, and his sadness for them was almost greater than their own. He knew all too well what it was like to be without anything in this world, and he had a sudden fear that his beloved Fathers might finish up as he had almost done, crawling the city streets in rags with begging bowls in their hands. And who would give to big-nosed foreigners? Who would give them anything but a kick and a curse of ill luck? Unbidden, there rose up in his mind the picture of Wang P'an's treasure house. One small coffer from its store would no doubt keep his Fathers for the remainder of their time in China. Wildly he thought that he knew how to get there, and then cold reason took him with the memory of the great rippling muscles and the long, gleaming swords of the guards. He sighed. But Wang P'an had it, and he knew someone in the House of Wang P'an. Did it have to be stolen?

"Can not the Excellency help you, my Father?" His desperate anxiety for them blotted out his manners, bringing him into the center of the group, his wide, concerned eyes moving from one to the other. "The Excellency has great treasure," he went on indiscreetly. "A whole room, a great marble room piled high with it, shimmering and glowing under the lamps."

Abashed, he stopped, and dropped his head, hands folding into his sleeves. Too late, he felt the three pairs of curious eyes on him, but it was Ri-ki who spoke, over-looking the rude interruption.

"And how do you know, Boy," he asked, "about the treasure of Wang P'an?" To the boy's intense relief, his voice was more amused than suspicious. Never, should he take to the pipe of opium himself, thought the boy, would he even dream of how I know.

Uneasily he said now, "It is the talk of all the bazaars."

He knew that he had satisfied the two priests, but Philip, ever suspicious and hostile, was glaring at him. He knew the gossip of the bazaars as well or better than the boy did, and the business of Wang P'an, the Father and Mother of his people, was not discussed. Fortunately the position was too serious for much notice to be taken of him. Father Ricci brushed him back to his corner with a gesture. In the small light of the bean oil lamp, his face was pale and anxious, seeing yet again the possibility of all his work for the souls of China foundering on the human, bodily need for money.

"There is but one thing to do, Michele," he said, pacing restlessly up and down the small room. "We have nothing left. There is nothing we can do here, so you must go back to Macao, Michele, taking Philip with you. You will need him on the journey. Go to our good friends there and tell them how our work is progressing. Tell them that our church is built, and our need is pressing to continue our work. I am sure they will not fail in this hour of need."

Father Ruggieri looked weary and dispirited, his big, handsome face heavy and a little mutinous.

"And when they ask me, Father," he said, "how many Christians we have baptized in China in this time, what shall I tell them?"

"You may tell them none," Matteo Ricci answered calmly. "But you may also tell them that that is not everything. Tell them that we have persuaded the Chinese to live with Christians in their midst, and that is the first great step. That is enough for this stage, Michele, after a thousand years when no foreigner has been allowed inside their walls. Is it not enough for you?" he added mildly.

The other priest sighed and looked abashed, but did not answer directly.

"When do you want me to go?" he asked.

"At once," Father Ricci answered. "At once. But I must first get permission from Wang P'an for your journey."

Wang P'an, when asked, gave more than his permission.

"He dare not give us money," Father Ricci explained on his return from the Governor's house. "He cannot be known to be buying the favor of the foreign bonzes. But he has loaned you a boat, Michele, for your journey, and two soldiers for your safe conduct to Canton. But we have in turn to do something for him."

"Worship Buddha?" asked Michele sardonically. He

did not have quite Matteo Ricci's faith in the integrity of Wang P'an.

"When you return, he wants you to bring him the materials for the making of a clock. He wishes to have one of his own, standing in his pavilions."

Father Ruggieri was relieved.

"And you had better look around, Michele, in the Mission House at Macao, for a picture of Our Lord. Somehow we must put an end to this idea that we worship a woman!"

Father Ruggieri smiled too, but he was not entirely content. When the day came for him to leave, and Wang P'an's soldiers stood outside the mission, warm in their quilted coats against the bright cold, he turned again to Father Ricci.

"The truth of it is, Matteo," he said, "I do not like leaving you alone for so many months. I do not feel that we have taught these Chinese anything, or that they like us any better than the day we came." He lifted a hand to stop Matteo from speaking. "Yes, I know you have the protection of Wang P'an, but can you be sure that if you are in trouble, you will get justice even from him? I have heard of the barbaric punishments he metes out."

"They are the punishments of all China," answered Father Ricci calmly. "Wang P'an only follows the penal code of his country, as is his duty as a magistrate. I am sure he would have to find me justly guilty of some crime before I suffered any of them."

The other priest did not look convinced, but shrugged and hitched his bundle of belongings onto his back. Matteo Ricci raised a hand in blessing as he watched the big, gray-robed figure walk steadily up the hill, leaving black footsteps in the frost, and towering above the two small, neat soldiers who marched in front, and over Philip at his side.

Silence settled on the tiny mission, and in the weeks that followed, Matteo Ricci began to think of the things that Michele had said to him before he left. In the quiet, with no one to speak with in his own tongue, he felt the vastness of China closing around him, oppressing him with its millions of souls to whom he seemed to draw no closer. They came still in great curious numbers to see the church, and like Wang P'an, they decided that it belonged to Buddhists; and with less courtesy than Wang P'an, they laughed their sides sore to see this foreign bonze worshiping a god that was a woman. Although his Chinese grew more fluent, Matteo Ricci found it impossible to find words to tell them differently. There were no such words in Chinese.

He brought the struggle down from the masses to the one, and did his best to explain to the boy what he did each day when he said his solitary Mass. The boy watched and listened, and heard a tongue that was not even the one the Fathers talked among themselves. When the Jesuit tried to explain it, the boy watched him with wide, devoted eyes, and struggled to understand simply because he loved the priest, and knew that it was his way of worshiping his God. But it seemed like the rituals of any other temple, and the great truths of Christianity clearly passed him by. The priest looked into his willing, empty eyes and knew a deep despair, however hard he might pray against it. When he could not reach this single child who loved him, how could he ever reach the unwilling thousands who did not listen? He looked at his gray robes and ran a hand over his shaven head, while the brush off the Chinese hills burned in his cooking stove and a bowl of rice cooled in his hand. He looked at the chopsticks that had become such second nature to him, and thought of the ease and routine now of his formal obeisances to Wang P'an. Dragging his quilted robe around him a little closer against the frosty December night, he asked his God if in truth, China had not taken him, before he had had the chance to take China.

The boy was unable to help his master's loneliness, but his thoughts were on help of another kind. If he could only lay hands on some of this great wealth belonging to the Mandarin, then the other Father could come back at once, and Ri-ki would not spend so many sad and solitary hours praying and talking to his clocks. There was only one person who could help him with this, and that was Chang, who seemed to have vanished completely. One night, the boy ventured so far as to follow the wall of Wang P'an's House out into the snow-covered fields, until he found the carved door, dark and complicated in the bright moonlight. Although he could see the whirls and curves of the carving quite clearly, and twisted his fingers in every direction as he had seen Chang do, the secret lock resisted him. In the end he ran, frightened by the loneliness and the cold moonlight and the howling of the wolves in the moon-blanched fields beyond the walls, and it was only when he felt safe again in the streets that he asked himself what he would have done if he had succeeded in getting inside. He remembered his sick terror with Chang that night, and he knew it would bring no money to his master to be sent his mutilated body on a pole. He could help him only by staying with him, and trying to make him happy by listening to all the things he said, even if he did not understand.

In a desperate effort to hold China at bay in his loneliness, Father Ricci made all he could of the Christian Christmas, and tried his best to tell the boy about the birth of Christ. This was not difficult. The Chinese tongue knew all the words of the farmyard and the stable, and it was simple enough to tell the ancient, glorious story of the baby born in a stable in a small land away to the west. The boy nodded happily. All this he could understand. A stable was nothing; the parents were lucky to have such shelter, and were far better off than the beggars of Macao. But when the priest tried to tell him that this Baby was the Lord of Heaven, and of the angels singing above the astonished shepherds, and of the wise men from his own eastern world, he stared at him in shocked disbelief.

"The Lord of Heaven was born in a stable?"

"Yes. He wished it so."

The boy's eyes flickered up to the picture of Our Lady in her blue robes, with the dazzle of light around her head; the Mother of the Lord of Heaven.

"His Father was a farmer?" he asked doubtfully.

"No. His Father was God Himself." He struggled. There were no words for the Trinity in Chinese, and if there were, could the boy understand them? "The Greatest Lord of Heaven," he said hopefully, and the boy accepted it.

"But why," he persisted, "did he allow his son to be born in a stable, and not in the Women's Courts of his House, as was proper to so great a Lord? Was it his First Son?"

"Yes."

Yet for all his master's careful story, the only impression that the boy gained of the Saviour's birth was that it was all very strange, and would have been far better managed in a Chinese House that was of such high standing. He could not begin to understand why the Greatest Lord of Heaven had been so careless as to allow his First Son to be born in a stable.

"It was," Father Ricci said patiently, "so that He might be poor and humble as other men."

"But, honorable Father, he was *not* poor or humble as other men. He was First Son to the Greatest Lord of Heaven, and in good Chinese families, this is a very important occasion, when the First Son is born."

136

He was too polite to argue much, or to refuse to believe. It was like the rain god; he bowed his acceptance of all he was told, and thought exactly as he had before. However, he thought it very suitable when the Jesuit gave him some cash and bade him go to the market for a good young duckling, and some lichees and pomegranates, for the birth of the Lord of Heaven should be celebrated on earth as well as in Heaven.

He went singing off up the hill, the embryo pigtail sticking out behind his head like a pothandle. He had been much distressed by this story about the stable, seeing it as a great loss of honor to the family to which he now belonged. The feasting to celebrate the birth of a son was much more as things should be, and his family pride was restored, so that he haggled in the marketplace with great confidence, coming away proudly with the plumpest duckling to be found in any basket.

At the door of the church he found Chang waiting for him, and almost dropped the duckling and ran to him, but with a great effort he controlled his pleasure.

"Ho, Young One," he said condescendingly, proudly conscious of his net full of goods, and the duckling flapping its white, helpless wings in his hand. "Have you been stealing into anyone else's house lately?"

Chang had been looking pale and subdued, waiting for the boy to greet him, but now a red, angry flush crept up his face and he gave no greeting in return.

"It was *my* House," he snapped.

"It was the House of Wang P'an," the boy said boldly,

"and what if I told of you creeping in there? They would slice you into little strips."

Chang did not seem unduly frightened by this.

"Who told *you*, slave, that it was the House of Wang P'an?"

"I followed the wall around to the gate," the boy said loftily. "You must think me very simple."

Now Chang stood and looked at him dumbly, and his face above the quilted cotton of his winter coat was small and pinched. The boy continued into his silence.

"And did you not hiss at me through the lattice when I was there on my master's important business? Did the servants of His Excellency know that you had crept in again?"

"It is *my* House," Chang said again obstinately, and then a fleeting grin crossed his face at the memory of pulling the small pigtail through the lattice.

The boy thought Chang was lying; he must at least be a servant in the house, but no more. He thought he saw an advantage, and a possible chance to help his beloved Fathers in their need.

"Prove it," he said contemptuously, "prove it, Young One! Prove that the House of Wang P'an is also your House!" His voice held a world of derision and stung Chang exactly as he had hoped.

"Have you not seen and heard me in there?" he cried angrily. "Did I not know my way about? What more proof do you want?"

The boy was almost beside himself with his own cunning, so that he eased his grip on the legs of the duckling and it nearly got away. When the flurry of struggling white feathers had died down, he turned triumphantly and made his point.

"Prove it to me by bringing me something from the treasure house of Wang P'an!"

Chang's reaction puzzled and confused him, and he did not understand it. A long moment the younger boy looked at him in amazement, and then his round face closed into an icy coldness.

"No," he said clearly, and said no more.

"Then I do not believe. It is not your House!"

The taunt did not seem to mean anything any more. Chang merely looked at him as if he hardly existed.

"It is nothing to me, slave, what you believe or what you do not. Do not ask again."

The boy was completely baffled. How could he understand that he had asked of Jade something that she would do for no one? For no one in the world would she so outrage the House of her beloved uncle.

The poor, puzzled boy could only know that somehow he had gone too far; had made some error, and lost face to this younger boy. Desperately he cast around for some way to restore it.

"You came to visit our Temple of the Lord of Heaven?" he asked kindly, as if the uncomfortable conversation had not happened.

Jade could not tell him now that she had come simply to see him because there was trouble for her in the

Women's Courts from which even Eldest Uncle could not save her. She had just wanted somebody to talk to, and had put on the green suit and the scarlet cotton coat, and slipped out to find the boy. Now she inclined her head graciously; any excuse would do.

"I have come to visit it," she said, as Chang.

The duckling now resigned and quiet in his hand, the boy led Chang proudly into the tiny church, soft with the light of lanterns, one small red lamp glowing at the altar, where candlelight fell on the fine painting of the Mother of the Lord of Heaven. Chang looked curiously all around him, and then dropped politely to his knees and bent his forehead to the ground in deep respect.

"I had been told," he said in astonishment as he got up again, "that your god was a woman, but truly to see it is to believe it."

"Who told you this foolish thing?"

"Someone that I know." Chang was evasive.

"Then they are wrong, not knowing of the Family of the Lord of Heaven."

Carefully he started on his own version of the story of the birth of Christ; telling Chang how the Greatest Lord of Heaven had gone on a lonely journey in a strange land, taking with him his wife. When they were far from shelter, his wife gave birth to a son, and there was nowhere for her to go except into a stable with the animals; but the Lord of Heaven was so important that even in this lonely stable musicians came to sing to the Eldest newborn Son, and from the nearest town three Mandarins came to bow down before him. It was to this great family, the boy finished ponderously, that he himself now belonged.

Chang did not seem very impressed.

"Like me," he said sadly. "Eldest—my relations are always telling me that I was born in a stable, when my parents were very poor. Did that baby's parents ever find him again?"

"The Lord of Heaven?" The boy was shocked. "His parents never left him. Would they, in so distinguished a family?"

"These things happen," Chang said, and his voice was still sad and heavy. "My brother went away, and my mother never found him again, even though the family came and found her, and brought us back to the Courts of my Father's Ancestors."

The boy did not pay him much attention. Whatever his remote connection with the House of Wang P'an, it was obvious that this Chang belonged to a family much inferior to the one which was now his own. Honor was completely restored.

"Such things," he said grandly, "could not happen in the Family of the Lord of Heaven."

He made a bold gesture and let go the legs of the duck. A few moments later Father Ricci came down the hill and saw the boy tearing frantically along the river bank after the white, fluttering shape of his Christmas Feast, fast followed by a strange child in a red coat.

141

He thought it important enough to say a small prayer of gratitude when the boy fell finally on top of its squawking, and recaptured it. Food had been scanty of late, and his stomach ached for the practical feasting of Christmas; nor was cash plentiful enough to replace their dinner, had it gone swimming off across the river.

By the time he reached the house the scared boy had tied the duckling's legs, and put it in a basket, and there was no sign of the other child in the bright scarlet coat.

9

Although she had failed to speak out about her trou-
bles, Jade had not gone down to the mission just for
adventure on this occasion. For several weeks the women
of the House had been talking behind their fans about
the shameful fact that she was already past the age of
marriage, and yet no suitable man had come to Wang
P'an to offer for her. The other mothers looked proudly
at their own silent and submissive daughters, tottering
through the pavilions on their tiny feet and making tinkling conversation about suitable things. Who, they
seemed to ask, could be expected to give good silver taels
and jade carvings and bales of silk for the privilege of
marrying this forward and talkative girl with her large
feet. The younger girls sniggered even more openly than
they had always done, and only the known love of Wang
P'an kept her from their open cruelty.

Now the time had come that a decision had been
made, and she must face the best bargain of a future
that they could find for her, valueless and unworthy as
she was. It took her all her self-control not to burst out
and scream at Eldest Aunt when she told her the name
of her future husband, not to weep and throw herself at

her feet, begging to be allowed to grow old unmarried rather than face life in the courts of the man they had chosen. He was the only one who had offered, wishing to gain favor with the Governor, and to say that he was ugly was not enough. He was also old, a gross, horrible creature with a face as white and shiny as the candles on the altar of the foreign priests, his overfed flesh bursting through the satin of his robes.

"Oh, no," was all she said, whispering, appalled. "Oh no, I cannot marry Lu Chin."

Eldest Aunt barely wasted her breath telling her how fortunate she was, fatherless, with no manners and her huge coolie's feet, that anyone should offer for her at all. It was settled and there was nothing more to be said. Jade gripped her hands in the warm lining of her sleeves until they hurt, and managed a formal bow of acceptance, her eyes as bleak as the snow-covered hills.

She wept that evening when she spoke of it with Wang P'an, who held her hot, unhappy hands with a most un-Chinese gesture of affection, looking at her with eyes as sad as her own. She was beautiful, his precious Jade, now that she was growing up, and more clever than the children of his own sons, but he could not fight all the habit and custom of his country for her, nor all the women of his House. So he had accepted the only offer she was likely to get. He himself had not approved of the merchant Lu Chin, knowing why he offered for his unmarriageable niece, but Eldest Aunt had insisted, and the affairs of the women were in her hands. Wang

P'an sighed. Who knew? Jade might prove to be better off in the ignorant courts of Lu Chin, than here where all the other women hated her.

He tried to distract her by telling her of the clock that he had ordered from the foreigners in Macao, that was to be brought back to him by the bonze who had gone there. Jade only wept again.

"My Uncle," she said, and shook her dark, shining head. "Oh, my Uncle, I will not be here to see it with you. Nor will there be clocks in the courts of Lu Chin."

Wang P'an fell silent, and they looked at each other sadly through her tears and found no more to say.

There was anxiety too down at the little mission house, anxiety that could be forgotten a while but not dispelled by the happy celebration of the Christian Christmas. In their movements around the town of Siuching, both Father Ricci and the boy had become aware of the mutterings and complaints that were being spread by the anti-Christians. The bonze Mi-kli, the whispers said, had not gone to Macao for any reasons given, but in order that he might return to invade China at the head of a Portuguese army. The foreign bonzes were no more than spies sent by Portugal for the overthrow of China. It was not true, they said, that the tower had anything to do with the Scholars, or with China. It was all part of the mission at its foot, and they were both part of a fortress from which the attack on China would be made. So the whispers circled the bazaars, and the ignorant listened in fear, and hostility grew toward the one lonely priest and his Chinese servant, in his tiny house beside the river.

Matteo Ricci listened wearily to the ridiculous stories and saw the fear growing in people's faces, and set himself all the more desperately to the task of learning to write, so that he might reach them with the written truth. Wang P'an lent him many books from his own fine library, long volumes beautifully handwritten or printed on finest rice paper, between soft covers, so that the book was carried like a scroll.

In the bazaars, the boy defended his masters fiercely, trying now to convince the people of the smallness and simplicity of the Mission in Macao. At first he was laughed at, and then as suspicion and hostility grew he was chased and threatened as a spy himself.

The year was still young, with bright, frosty days, and the night sky was still spangled with the fireworks of the long celebrations of the Chinese New Year, when word came at last from Macao. But it was not Father Ruggieri, nor Philip, who arrived, but a strange Indian, coming back with the two soldiers and followed through the town by a curious and excited crowd. As he came to the mission the crowd drew back, unwilling to come closer, but convinced that the coming of this strange, dark-faced man was proof of all they had feared. Where was the bonze Mi-kli, who had gone away with these soldiers? Was he not, as the gossip said, gathering an army in Macao to attack Siuching? And this dark-skinned one was undoubtedly a Portuguese soldier of high rank, ready to meet Mi-kli when he arrived at the head of his victorious troops.

The Indian was no more than a harmless clockmaker, sent by Michele, who had not returned himself as he had been unable to raise any money as yet. He had sent the Indian with the parts of Wang P'an's clock, so that their good will with the Mandarin might not suffer. Wang P'an showed himself delighted that Mi-kli had so thought of him when Father Ricci took the man to his house, and ordered two of his best metal workers to help with the construction of the clock.

But that night, the first stone was thrown, to smash from the top of the tower down through the fragile tiles of the mission roof below it.

The boy and the priest jumped as the heavy crash came from above their heads, loud and threatening above the intermittent crackle of the distant firecrackers. The small building shook, and the brush in Father Ricci's hand jerked across his precious stretch of paper, blotting the painstaking characters and slopping the ink in its china pot.

"What was that, my Father?"

The priest did not stop to answer him, pausing only to lay aside the brush before rushing out into the cold darkness, with the boy scuttling after him. The moon was waning from the full, the slow decline of the month-long festival, and from above the town showers of colored sparks lifted to the sky, and the faint smoky haze held the acrid smell of gunpowder. But in the

147

darkness around the mission, and around the tower behind it, there was silence. The priest and the boy ran here and there, searching for what had happened; rushing together again to question each other's puzzled faces in the chilly moonlight.

"Nothing," said the boy. "Nothing. I can find nothing and no one."

"It was not no one," said Father Ricci shortly. "Nor was it the devil thumping on my roof!"

In his pacing, he felt fragments of something on the ground under his soft Chinese shoes.

"Ah," he said, stooping to gather them in his fingers. In the lamplight they showed themselves to be the broken remnants of his roof tiles. "Ah," he said again, "I did not think it was the devil. And there is only one place from where anyone could throw a stone large enough to smash our tiles."

"The tower," said the boy.

"The tower. I can't believe that the proud Scholars would throw a stone themselves, but they have not stopped someone else from doing it."

The boy looked desperately troubled, but at the moment there was only one thing that he could think to do. Hands in his blue, quilted sleeves, he bowed with great formality.

"I beg the Father to forgive," he said anxiously, "the ill manners of my ignorant countrymen."

Wang P'an himself could not have been more dignified, and the priest smiled at him and bade him go to sleep and not trouble himself further, but the cold, snow-weighted morning showed them that their suspicions were correct. The stone had fallen on the roof of the church, lodged in the rafters in the middle of their shattered roof tiles, and the snow had drifted through the ragged hole to lie in a white, chilly drift along the floor. When the Scholars came, later in the day, the Jesuit confronted them indignantly. His careful Chinese-like calm was gone, and his anger was all warm Italian. They looked at him with their black eyebrows raised under their buttoned hats, and drew aside their purple robes, showing clearly their distaste for his crude bad manners and loud voice, and the eldest told him coldly that they knew nothing of the things he mentioned. There was no more sympathy in the town, where the people were still silent and hostile because the second bonze had not yet returned. In the bitter cold of the turning year, Father Ricci and the boy had to climb the snow-laden roof and mend it as best they could with their own frozen fingers.

There were no more actual incidents in the weeks that followed, and they grew used to the cold eyes and averted faces of the people of the town, Father Ricci drawing comfort only from the attitude of Wang P'an. The Mandarin looked at everything with the eyes of truth and reason, and was not swayed either by wild stories or by superstition. His soldiers had returned to him from Macao with the Indian clockmaker, and laughed out loud at the tales of an army massing there to invade Siuching. As a reassurance to the lonely and harassed priest, Wang P'an showed him a mark of the greatest favor at the time of the Festival of Ming Ching, when the Mandarin ploughed the first formal furrow in the soft red earth. The season of planting had begun, in all the flat lands and the small terraced fields of the hills and the wide wet stretches of the rice fields.

"It is our custom," Wang P'an said to Father Ricci on the occasion of a visit to inspect the clock, "to gather every member of our families together at this feast, and to make pilgrimage to pay our respects at the Shrines of our Ancestors. It might be that you will do me the honor of walking in my procession to these ceremonies, to witness the oldest of our Chinese customs."

The Jesuit bowed deeply. In spite of the polite words of the invitation, there was no doubt that it was a command. Wang P'an's procession would be the largest and noisiest and most gorgeous of them all, and only the very privileged were invited to join it. Although keeping his face calm and polite, as he was learning always to do, the priest was filled with secret pleasure. The Chinese habit of worshiping their ancestors was the thing that troubled him most when thinking of leading them to God. It was difficult enough to turn men away from idols, but how much more to turn them away from their own dead! What an opportunity to see for himself how much it meant to them.

He told the boy later in the day that he was to come with him.

"Me?" The boy's eyes widened in astonishment and not a little fear. "Me? To go to the Ancestor Ceremonies of the Excellency?"

"Who else?" the priest asked him. "I cannot walk alone in the procession of Wang P'an like a poor man without a servant. It would not be respectful to the Lord of Heaven whom I represent."

He felt a pang of pity seeing the boy's agitated face, thinking it to be caused by having to face these ceremonies in other families when he had no family himself. He reproached himself a little that he had given no thought to inquiring about the boy's family since they had been in China, but China was so large and he had so very much to do.

"Together," he said to him now, "we will walk as the Family of the Lord of Heaven, among all these other families."

The boy bowed, knowing that the priest tried to be kind to him, but the gesture was automatic, for his troubles were not as the priest thought them. The boy was frightened of Chang. He had put him into a sweating fear of death, pulling his pigtail that day through the lattice. If he were anything at all in Wang P'an's household he would be there for these ceremonies. Everybody went, except the very ancient and the babies, even the women were carried in their swaying palanquins to the Temple of Ancestors, and then tottered on their tiny feet to do their ritual weeping and laying out of food and flowers and joss sticks for the dead. Chang was certain to be somewhere in the procession, and what foolishness might he not think up? The boy shivered, almost feeling the hand on his small pigtail, stretching his neck for the ax.

The Jesuit watched his troubled face and shook his head, amazed at the importance that the Chinese attached to pride, and especially to pride of family. To a man who had given up pride and family, and all his possessions gladly for the service of his God, it was not to be understood.

The boy was by nature too cheerful to worry deeply on his problem. He had soon decided that on the day he would just have to deal with whatever might happen, and a few days before the festival he grinned happily at his master over his rice bowl, listening to the first fireworks crackling in the distance.

"My Father," he said, "I have been thinking about these feasts. We are indeed lucky to be members of the Family of the Lord of Heaven."

"We are indeed," Father Ricci replied. "But why do you think so?"

"At the New Year, we did not have trouble with the Kitchen God, running off up to the Jade Emperor of Heaven with all his stories of what we had done wrong."

"The Kitchen God?" he asked, and then could not resist adding, "brother to the Rain God?"

The boy firmly ignored his joke.

"Yes, honored Father, did you not know? Every household has a Kitchen God, and for the last ten days of the Old Year it is his duty to go to the Jade Emperor of Heaven and report on the family he lives with. So for those ten days, the families paste paper across his mouth so that he cannot talk!"

The priest nodded. "I have heard of the Kitchen God," he said, "and you are right. He is no trouble to us. We have to answer directly ourselves to the Lord of Heaven for everything we do. There is no one to spy on us."

"Directly?" The boy laid down his rice bowl, and his face blazed with excitement. "My honored master means that one day we will see the Lord of Heaven for ourselves and answer for everything we do?" He was enchanted at the thought of really seeing the Eldest of his Family for himself, and he hoped desperately that it could be arranged for Chang to see him too. The priest looked at his face, and knew that again, somehow or other, Christian thought had not gotten straight into the Chinese mind.

"Yes," he said simply to the shining face. "Yes. One day you will see Him. Now our rice is cooling, so let us eat."

The boy was well satisfied. He would be able to look more calmly on the might and splendor of Wang P'an now that he knew that sometime he would walk in the procession of the Eldest of his own Family, and could hope for Chang to see him.

The day of the feast was clear and brilliant, the sun rising in a blaze of scarlet over the rounded hills, flushing all the tender colors of the young growth. All the households were astir early, especially the women, who made all the last preparations for the feasting, and opened the pigskin chests to take out folded, precious clothes of ceremony for their menfolk.

Neither Father Ricci nor his servant had any special clothes, but did their best to clean and tidy the shapeless gray robe and blue cotton suit before they took their place as bidden in the procession that was forming in the Outer Court of the Mandarin. The vast area was massed with people, being thrust here and there by fussing Chamberlains in scarlet coats, who were trying to settle everyone in order of importance. Every single outlying member of Wang P'an's huge family was there in the enormous chattering crowd, from the rich in their bright silks with servants running at their carrying poles to the poor retired servants and their children and their children's children, unable in their poverty to provide a family feast of their own, but given one by the unfailing generosity of Wang P'an, the Father and Mother of them all.

The Chamberlain seemed very troubled as to where to place the Jesuit in the procession, looking with his crinkled eyes at the tired gray robe, and then down at the scroll of precedence in his hands. Finally he placed him at the very end of the rich part of the procession, behind the silks and palanquins but before the blue cotton block of the walking poor. Matteo Ricci smiled to see his place in China so carefully marked, and then he and the boy took their positions and waited to see the immediate Household procession of the Mandarin.

The train of trumpets and cymbals and great bronze gongs was even larger then usual, followed by outriders in golden coats on small curveting horses from Mongolia, and the usual crowd of barefoot, running guards threatening with the crack of their long whips. Then came Wang P'an, sitting like a waxen image of himself in his open litter, wearing the bright, embroidered robes of festival and not moving a muscle of his face as his whole dependent family bowed before him. The boy risked death by twitching up his eyes even before the Mandarin was past, lest he miss seeing even one of those who might be in his train. Carefully he watched, from the splendid mounted nobles who rode immediately behind the litter, down to the throng of servants who pressed together, marching at the back; but there was no sign of Chang.

It was curious. Chang seemed so free in the household, and came to no harm for it, yet on this day when the Excellency should have mustered everyone who served him to walk in this procession, he was nowhere to be seen. It might be that he was a kitchen boy, and was left behind to tend the pots? That could not be so. Kitchen boys did not speak the purest Mandarin.

He stopped thinking about it as another blast of trumpets and clash of gongs heralded the approach of the women of the House of Wang P'an, even more heavily guarded and surrounded than was the Governor himself. The palanquins came swaying into sight around the inner screen, one after another of them, and all of them gold and scarlet with close-drawn silken curtains, and curling golden dragons on the roof. All of them were exactly the same as the one that he had seen before, so that he had no idea now whether even that girl was there, never mind Chang. Behind them ran the servants who carried the baskets and bundles of food, and flowers and joss sticks to be left for the Ancestors. When the last guard had passed, the Chamberlains hustled the people of the crowded court into their positions behind, and the long, unwieldy procession of Wang P'an straggled out through the streets of the city and out into the springtime countryside, along the bamboo walks above the rice fields and the high paths beside the canals.

It was a long march, and everywhere they looked there were similar processions, winding along the canal banks or trailing through the sunken roads. They were of all stations, from the bright colors and palanquins of the rich, through the poorer merchants who pushed their wives in wheelbarrows, down to the country poor, whose women trudged along beside the men, with feet unbound, large and ugly as those of Jade herself.

Every procession pressed aside and made room for that of Wang P'an, the people dropping on their faces to venerate it as it passed, but gradually the number of processions thinned out as they began to stop at their tombs, scattered haphazardly over the wide, flat fields. Only that

of the Mandarin was left in the end, winding and banging and ringing its bells across the flat land to where the curved points of a roof lifted sharp on the blue sky, above the tombs of his Honorable Ancestors.

The Memorials of the close family of Wang P'an himself were in the vast central pagoda, with its painted walls and wide, looping roof of pale green tiles, standing in the dark shadows of high, close-growing pines. To the Jesuit's surprise a servant came to him, and told him that it was the Mandarin's wish that he should come inside and see the ceremonies close at hand. The boy followed closely at his master's heels into the huge, shadowy spaces of the pagoda, where the chill of winter still seemed to hang in the dark air. Even Wang P'an did not concern himself much with the state of his tombs on any day but this, and cobwebs hung about the painted roof beams; piles of rubbish were pushed into the corners, and the highest shadows of the pointed roof were swishing with disturbed and angry bats.

Once again the boy craned his neck watching for Chang as the Mandarin led his family in from the far end of the pagoda. They came in order of their seniority, to kneel in ranks before the long wall that held all the memorial tablets of the honored dead of their dynasty; in front of them was the platform underneath the tablets, where they would lay their offerings of food and flowers and printed prayers for the welfare of the dead; and where the tall, gilded tripods would lift their perfumed smoke from the heaped joss sticks when all the worshipers were gone, the flowers dead, and the food taken by the beggars who waited outside among the trees.

One by one the boy looked at the boys of all ages who walked in proud procession in the ranks of the family, but no one of them was Chang. The women came in next, tottering helplessly on their tiny feet, and held up under the arms by their servants, and he lowered his eyes respectfully as was proper, but could not resist glancing up under his lashes. No one ever saw a Chinese woman of a noble house, except on such an occasion as this, and even this was private almost to the family itself. The last girl in the tottering procession caught his interest, because she walked alone, needing no help, and trying uncomfortably to match her large, unbound feet to the steps of the other women. Good manners told him not to stare, but even he, a beggar from the streets of Macao, knew that this was not usual in a lady of such a household. From under his lowered lids he looked again curiously, careful lest he should be noticed to be watching her. The girl wore a beautiful embroidered coat of sea green satin, of the same shifting green that he had seen in the ocean off Macao on a clear spring day. Under the stiff hem of the gown, the big agile feet looked strange and awkward, as though they belonged to a boy. To a boy! The boy's heart gave a sick, sudden lurch, and felt as if it landed somewhere else in his chest, making it difficult to breathe. The cool, windy pagoda seemed suddenly to have grown intolerably hot.

"No," he told himself firmly. "No! It could not be done!"

When he felt he dared, and could control his uneven breath, he looked at her again, staring at those large, unlikely feet. All the women were kneeling now, banging their foreheads on the floor and weeping; the noisy, formal weeping that was proper to the occasion, filling the dark musty air with stricken cries of grief for people they had never even known. The girl knelt not far away, and with her was a woman who seemed to be her mother. They were opposite two tablets toward the end of the wall, and alone out of all the women they were not wailing. As if, thought the boy with sudden understanding, they truly have something to grieve for. But it was dark in the pagoda, and they stood in shadow; however he might strain his eyes, he could see no more to confirm his sudden, terrified suspicion.

Then the bright spring sun moved around, and fell suddenly through the spaces of a lattice straight upon the girl, who lifted her sad face a moment to blink in the unexpected light. Instantly the boy knew, and felt petrified with the terror of his knowledge. There was no coat of plain green cotton, but a long robe of sea green, crusted with pearls in the silver threads of its embroidery; no thick pigtail hanging to the waist, but black hair neatly coiled, catching the light in its shining folds, with a scarlet flower tucked into it above one ear. Satin slippers on the big, free feet. The boy Chang, with whom he had talked so freely, was a girl, and one of the close family of Wang P'an!

The Governor was intoning the prayers to the dead Ancestors in his calm, measured voice, and the sweet, heady incense of the joss sticks was creeping through the shadows. The boy felt hot and sick with fright, tempered with a spurt of anger that this girl had so used him, and so deceived him, putting him in danger of his life. The most terrible deaths in China were kept for those who in any way dared violate the privacy of the Women's Courts. And he had been with this girl in her house even while she was dressed as a boy!

He remembered how he had asked her to steal the Mandarin's treasure, and the heart that had been in his chest now leaped up into his throat and threatened to choke him. He did not dare look at her again, vaguely aware through a haze of fear of the rest of the ceremonies and the long procession leaving the Pagoda of the Dead. He only came to his senses again when he realized that his master was speaking to him.

"I have spoken twice already," he said. "Are you deafened with the gongs and cymbals? I want you to ask the Chamberlain if it is allowed for me to look at the Ancestor Tablets of Wang P'an."

The Chamberlain allowed it with pride, glad to allow the ignorant foreigner to survey the glory of the House of his Master. Because it was the nearest, the first tablet they looked at was the one before which the girl had bowed with her mother. The boy had to shake his head

161

to clear his hazy eyes before he could read it for the priest.

"Wang Jang-fu," he read slowly. "Youngest Brother to Wang P'an." He added the date of his death, which was inscribed on the tablet underneath the name.

Then he read the smaller tablet underneath.

"Wang-fu. Son to Jang-fu." He turned to the priest in surprise. "It does not say when he died," he said. "How could it not, if he is among the Ancestors?"

Father Ricci did not pay attention. He was moving on to the larger and more ornate tablets. But the boy did not move on, continuing to stand in the shaft of sunlight that had fallen on the girl, looking at the small tablet of Wang-fu.

It was dark before they got back to the mission house, the sudden, warm, humming darkness of the Chinese spring. Before they could light their lamps they stumbled over the broken tiles that littered their tiny court, and inside the living room they found the clear stars shining through a hole in the roof, and in the middle of the floor the huge rock which had made it.

10

The Feast of Ming Ching was over, the celebrations fin-
ished, and the bare red earth of the hills already green
with the first crops of the year. The minds of the people
were less occupied, and they turned back to their hostile
thoughts against the mission, fanned in their feelings by
the Scholars who were determined to drive the Jesuits
from Siuching.

The rock that had come crashing through the roof
while Father Ricci and the boy were at the feast was only
the first of many during the following days. The assail-
ants came only at night with their dead thump of destruc-
tion, and no matter how fast Father Ricci moved there
was never anyone to be seen.

"Honored Father," the boy said to him anxiously. "We
will never catch them by running out when the rock is
thrown. We must hide and catch them as they do it!"

The priest was irritable and impatient, annoyed by the
senseless persecution even when he had the protection of
Wang P'an, and tired and depressed by the long, lonely
winter he had passed with no one of his kind to speak
with; feeling China closing around him in her immense
size and self-certainty; worrying and wondering whether

he could hold out until Michele came back with some money, and often worrying whether he could hold out at all against the great pressure simply to become Chinese. It troubled him that they had not made one single convert, in spite of his assurances to Michele that it did not matter.

Now he lifted exasperated eyes from the clock he tuned and regulated for the Governor.

"Wait for them!" He was angry. "Why should I waste my time waiting for them? I have better things to do."

Even as he spoke, he wondered despondently what other things he had to do, among a people who would pay no attention to anything he might have to say to them. Anxiously the boy watched his harassed face, and determined that if the Father would not help himself, then he would have to help him. His heart gave a little bump of fear. He did not know who it was who threw the stones at night. How many were there? He might just earn a slit throat for himself, and be no help to Ri-ki. Then he almost shrugged. He lived in such perpetual fear of what might happen if that girl came near him again, that his master's enemies were a small terror beside it. The Father had need of his help, and that was enough, so on the same evening he began his watch, slipping out as soon as he had laid the rice bowl before his master, and the quick spring dusk had darkened the river and the hills. For two long nights he watched and saw nothing, gaining no more for himself than weary, yawning days, and plenty of time in the silent darkness to think about his own fears and problems.

On the third night he crouched in the shadows of the mission wall where he could see the entry to the tower. He was so deep in thought over all their troubles that he almost did not notice the small, quiet shadow creeping up toward the tower, slipping through the milky darkness of the starlit night. The boy's eyes were used to the dark, and he could see quite clearly the figure that ignored the doorway of the tower, and proceeded to climb nimbly up the sides of it, using the carvings of the stonework and railings for a grip. Across his back, a sling held some burden, and the boy had no doubt as to what it was. His own troubles forgotten, he grinned with pleasure in the darkness. The figure climbing so briskly up the tower was no bigger than he was himself; there should be no trouble here, especially if he was taken by surprise. The intruder was silhouetted a moment against the flood of starlight at the top of the tower, and then almost at once, a rock crashed down into the roof of the church.

With a great outcry, Matteo Ricci burst from the house and rushed to the door of the tower.

"Come down," he shouted. "Come down, evil one! I am waiting for you!"

"Ah, yes, my poor Father," said the boy to himself. "That is what you do every time, and he is going to come down, the evil one, but not the way you think!"

He did not call to the furious, shouting priest, but crept silently around to the far side of the circular tower.

Here its base lay shadowed by a grove of peach and magnolia trees, ready to waft their perfume through the high thoughts of the Scholars when they sat under the tower roof, contemplating the moon. Now the boy crept in among their gnarled trunks and lifted his face to the stonework of the tower, grinning a little as he heard what he expected. A moment later he was sitting on the rock thrower's head, having jumped him in the instant his feet touched the ground.

"My Father!" he bellowed then, joyfully. "My Father, I have him! Come quickly, I have him!"

The priest rushed around the base of the building and dragged the intruder to his feet in the tangle of roots.

"Evil creature!" he shouted in Italian, no Chinese being equal to his anger. "Evil wretch, so to destroy the House of God!"

He shook the Chinese like a puppy in his big hands. In turn the Chinese poured out floods of abuse that only the boy could understand. Dragged around into the light of the lamp above the gate, he proved to be a youth of eighteen or so, but so undersized that he was no bigger than the boy, and under the gate arch they stood in a furious, noisy huddle. The Chinese youth, helpless in the priest's grip, yelled his abuse and accusations; the priest poured out torrents of furious Italian, and the boy, understanding the Chinese, yelled at him not to speak so to the honored Father. It was some time before they were calm enough to realize that they were no longer alone. In the shadows of the starlight and the small lamplight, the pale,

shocked faces of three old Mandarins looked at them in
horror.

"What can be so troubling our honored visitor?" the
eldest asked, as calmly as his dignity demanded, trying to
make his gentle old voice heard above the still shouting
Chinese. He had been to the mission with Wang P'an,
and had nothing but admiration for the scholar from the

West. Father Ricci was too angry to speak any Chinese, still breathing heavily and shaking the culprit by the back of the neck. It was the boy who recovered himself, bowing deeply and explaining in his best tones that this malefactor had been caught up the tower, throwing rocks through the roof of the mission.

The three pale, elderly faces were more shocked than ever.

"Our most humble apologies to the foreign scholar," the eldest said, "that any of our people should be so ignorant as to do this. But tell your master, boy, that it serves no good to try and deal with the wrong himself. Tell him to bring the culprit before the Governor."

Anxiously, because he thought him right, the boy repeated what the old man had said, but Father Ricci was too exasperated to listen.

"No," he said. "No." He was speaking now a mixture of Chinese and still furious Italian. "I will deal with him myself. In here first, to cool himself, while I think what I shall do."

Ahead of him he forced the babbling youth to the door of their small storehouse, and thrust him inside.

"Let him stay there a while, and think on what he has done!"

The three ancients shook their round, capped heads.

"Tell your master," the eldest said again, above the shouting and pummeling on the storehouse door. "Tell your master that it is not wise. Tell him, boy, that he only makes trouble for himself."

But Matteo Ricci was past listening, and past the careful use of Chinese patience, worn with the effort of mending the roof almost daily, and with his nagging anxiety about Father Ruggieri and the quest for money.

"I will face whatever trouble may come," he cried, and without even the careful courtesy of exchanging bows he turned and went into his house, closing the door behind him even on the boy, as though in that weary and exasperated moment the sight of even one more Chinese face was more than he could bear.

The three old Mandarins looked after him and then shrugged and went on their dignified way to some evening gathering where they might read their poems or display a painting, and talk for hours over some fine shade of meaning in a word, wreathed in the perfumed smoke of their weathered pipes. The boy looked after them and sighed, for how could he hope to bring the Father to see wisdom by himself? He knew, without these Ancient Ones to tell him, that there could be great trouble for his master for locking up a Chinese, but he dared not try to let the youth out himself.

He sat down under the wall of the mission, thinking to keep out of his master's way until this rare temper had cooled, and watch too to see what happened about this fellow. He may have friends who would come to look for him, and not be as small and unarmed as he was himself. The Father may be in danger from them. The boy wished that the huge Mi-kli were here to protect his master; he was big enough to handle half a dozen Chinese.

Through the evening many passers-by stopped, halted by the muffled cries that poured from behind the door of the storehouse. The boy kept himself in the shadow and listened to their talk, groaning to think of all the tales that would be going round Siuching by morning. If they came to Wang P'an's ears and he was to believe them, then the Father would be on the boat back to Canton in no time at all.

The young moon paled in the white light of the stars and the night grew late. Fewer people were passing by, and the cries from the storehouse had died into silence. He wondered if he dared go in and brave this anger of his Father, to try and persuade him to let the youth go, but temper in Ri-ki was so rare that it had frightened him. He stayed where he was, to wait patiently until the anger had spent itself, and the Father came out once more himself, at peace with his spirit. Then he could talk to him.

He drowsed a little, thinking longingly of his warm quilt on the top of the stove, and woke with a start to see another small shadow creeping along the mission wall quite close beside him, making for the tower.

Another of them, he thought, and another small one! This one I will take myself and silently, and then the Father will not get himself into more trouble. The small shadow crept past him and did not see him, intent only on not being seen itself. Smiling a little, the boy followed, stalking it no more than a pace away until the moment came to jump.

He knew there was something wrong the moment he brought the figure down. It collapsed too easily, soft and yielding, giving no more than a frightened squeak underneath the hand he thrust across its mouth, instead of a stream of curses like the other boy. A buttoned cap rolled off and the black pigtail gleamed in the lamplight. The boy seized it and used it to pull the head around in the dust until he could see the face. Then he could not get fast enough to his feet, sick and appalled at what he had done.

"Chang," he stammered desperately, and knew that that was wrong. "Honorable . . ." He did not even know what to call her, for there were no rules for speaking to noble girls when you had just rolled them in the dust in the street. He could do no more than bow and bow and bow again, almost gibbering apology for what he had done.

Jade scrambled to her feet, ramming the small, dusty cap back on to her tousled hair, thinking happily that she would look a little less respectable now in the mean streets.

"Who told you?" she demanded fiercely. She had no time for the courtesies, nor did she care. "Who told you who I am? Stop that bowing, boy, for I am only Chang to you."

"You are not Chang to me! How can you be? Do you not know—do you not realize?" He could find no words to speak to her of the enormity of what she was doing. A high-born Chinese lady, out in the streets of the town in a boy's clothes! There was no name for the crime of anyone found helping her to do this; only death, and a most terrible death at that. She did not listen to him.

"Who told you?" she demanded again, for the moment almost as frightened as he, for who could have found out to tell this foreigner's slave?

"I saw you," he said. "I saw you for myself, at the Temple of the Ancestors, where I waited on my master. The Excellency invited him to watch the ceremonies. I noticed your feet," he could not help adding.

"Ah," she said, with a long breath of relief. "My feet! Everybody notices my feet, but at last they have proved useful, to get me out of that cage that is the House of my uncle. So no one else knows but you? You did not tell the bonze your master?"

"How could I? He would send me back at once to Macao, lest I imperil his mission. And you must go away from here at once. At once!" Like her, he had forgotten courtesy and rank in the urgency of the moment; two anxious children interested in nothing but their own troubles. "Go away! Do you not realize that it is death for me to speak to you like this? And death to the mission of my honorable Fathers who have given me life?"

She was silent, and in her silence his fear of the noble lady of the Mandarin's House left him. She was only a girl, and a bit younger than himself, and doing something very, very foolish.

He saw the movement of her nod in the darkness.

He started to say that he would go back with her as

far as the gate, and then he thought better of it. "I will not come with you, then if you are caught, the trouble is for yourself alone, and you are of the Governor's House."

He thought of the dark streets that she must pass through, and felt a prick of shame to let her go alone, but firmly he made himself think of his masters. They had given him life, and their mission must come first. By the great toe of Buddha, this girl offered him nothing but death!

"Go," he hissed to her, but to his infinite dismay she did not go.

He felt some new quality in her silence, and without a word she slid down beside the wall and buried her face in her hands. He could feel, rather than see, the desperate sobbing that shook her. Helplessness took him, and he stared down at her and wildly all around him, terrified that someone would pass by. Clumsily then he knelt down beside her, touched to some sick misery to see her weeping so. He did not understand himself, having only just found out that she was a girl, and knowing nothing of them; but there was something about the small, crouching figure with the tendrils of ruffled hair, and the lamplight catching the gleam of tears between her fingers, that touched him almost to rage that anyone should make her so unhappy.

"Come," he said, rough and embarrassed, trying to hide his pity. "Do you want me sliced, weeping here in the lamplight? Come around into the shadows underneath the trees and tell me why you cry."

He took the hot, damp hand that she put trustingly into his, and he had a curious feeling as if some small, gentle bird had come down from the trees and rested in his fingers. For the moment he had forgotten about Wang P'an and the threat of death. In the dark shadows of the magnolias, in the smell of ancient bark and long dead flowers, he sat her down and waited patiently until the fierce weeping snuffled into silence, and she sat up straight and thrust back her ruffled hair. He saw her hands moving small and white in the darkness and wondered why he had never noticed that they did not suit a boy.

"I came to you for help," she said. "You must not send me away."

But I must, the boy thought. I must send you away or die myself in the end, for someone is bound to find out in time.

Aloud, he asked her why she came to him, poor slave of the bonzes. What could he do for a girl from the House of Wang P'an?

"My uncle." She answered his unspoken question. "Wang P'an is my Eldest Uncle. I live with him because my Father, who was his Youngest Brother, is dead."

"Wang Jang-fu," the boy said, remembering the tablet on the wall in the House of Ancestors.

She did not seem surprised that he knew.

"Yes," she said. "Jang-fu. I do not remember him."

"And his son, Wang-fu?" he asked, thinking of the second tablet.

"I do not know. I just do not know. Wang-fu was my Elder Brother, and were he here I would not be a thing of no value, having no man of my own in my family."

Her voice was rising again and choking with tears, but she calmed herself with an effort and told him all she knew of the family quarrel, and the death of her father far from his home.

"But all that is long ago," she said desperately, "and now I am the daughter of a widow, with no brothers, and of no value to anyone. Not even Eldest Uncle can save me from Eldest Aunt giving me in marriage to the horrible Lu Chin!"

He jumped up in his shock, never noticing the crash of his head on the gnarled branches of the magnolias, staring at her in the shadows. Lu Chin! He had seen Lu Chin himself often enough, swaying through the bazaars on the bent shoulders of his carriers, with his great, grubby satin bulk overflowing the sides of his palanquin and his stubby fingers picking endlessly at the piled sweetmeats in his lap. This small, clean, soft-faced creature, boy or girl, could not be given into the household of Lu Chin! As he looked at her, ferocity and anger gave way to the knowledge of his absolute helplessness. He raised his hands in a futile gesture and for a moment he was very near to tears himself.

"What can I do?" he asked her hopelessly. "What can I do?"

She was very quiet now, her voice soft and hopeless, as gentle and feminine as Eldest Aunt could wish her to be.

"I did not think," she said, "that truly you could do anything. But I had most desperate need to talk to someone, and in my home I have no one but my dearest Eldest Uncle, and he is as grieved over it as I am myself. But I know he cannot help it, and so he will not talk of it, and we talk of all things except this one. But he told me something."

"Yes?"

"He told me that your master told him something; that in the western lands he comes from, men have only one wife and no more. Now, Lu Chin already has a wife, so by the laws of your bonzes, he could not take another."

"So?"

"So nothing at all, I suppose." Her voice was dead. "There is no hope that your bonze could make Lu Chin worship his god before the moon is full, and follow his laws."

Together they looked up through the tangled tracery of magnolia branches to the young, arrogant moon, riding the springtime sky with all the promise of the soft young season. The boy did not even need to answer her, sick with his certainty that there was nothing he could do to help her. Sick too with the sadness of loss, that once the moon was full and she was in the courts of Lu Chin, he would never see her again; either as the impudent young Chang, or as the smiling girl in jewel-crusted silks, stealing a forbidden glance out through the curtains of her palanquin.

176

"I will ask," he said, hopefully, suddenly. "I will ask my honored Father about these things. I know that he is much admired by Excellency Wang P'an. Who knows what he may be able to say to him to turn his thoughts?"

Jade shook her head.

"He admires your master very much," she said, "and his mind is open to many of his foreign thoughts. But no one may speak to him of the private affairs of his House."

The boy was silent, knowing this to be true.

"But I will talk to him just the same," he said stoutly, to give her hope. "My master is very clever. He may be able to talk to the Eldest Uncle so that it does not appear to offend him."

At that moment, the banging and shouting in the storehouse began again, and Jade leaped to her feet in alarm, groping in the shadows for her cap.

"What is that? Who makes that noise?"

The boy explained to her that his master had caught the youth early in the evening, and shut him up a while to teach him a lesson.

"He will let him out soon," he said, thinking of what she might say to Wang P'an, then remembering that she dared say nothing.

But Jade was frightened. "The noise," she said. "The noise. Someone might come to see what it is. I am going now. I thank you," she added as sweetly as if she sat in Wang P'an's pavilion, "for talking with me."

"No," said the boy. "Don't go." It was suddenly intolerable that he could not help her, that she should run back now to the house and family that would at the full moon dispatch her to Lu Chin.

At that moment his master called him from the gate of the court, and he stood irresolute, turning from one to the other. Jade crammed her cap down onto her tousled hair, and without another word turned and ran away into the darkness. There was nothing he could do but watch her go. Slowly and sadly he answered his master and went toward the square of light that was the open gate.

"He is still shouting," the priest said, but the boy could see that the fire of his Father's temper had died, and he was once more his calm and quiet self.

"Will you let him out now?" he asked anxiously. There were lights, and obviously people, coming along the road past the tower.

Father Ricci was not yet as calm as he seemed.

"It will do him no harm to stay a little longer," he said sharply.

But the lights along the road proved to belong to the servants of the three old Mandarins, who were returning from their evening of words and music. They paused on hearing the cries still coming from the storehouse, and spoke earnestly together, three old heads leaning close with wisps of white hair escaping from the diminished pigtails that hung down behind. The eldest turned and bowed deeply to the priest.

"Tell your foreign master," he said to the boy, "that we cannot warn him urgently enough that he harms himself by what he does. He will never have the goodwill of the people of Siuching if things happen such as this." He clasped his thin old hands anxiously in his sleeves and went on.

"We have seen what has occurred, and know the truth, but others have not and will make up their own stories, for our people are ignorant and there are many things they do not understand."

The boy repeated it all carefully to Matteo Ricci, now thoughtful.

"I am, my Elders," the priest said, "but an ignorant foreigner, angered by the ill manners of this youth. But I will do as you say, and agree that he has had enough punishment."

He handed the boy the key to the storeroom, and the instant the door opened the youth shot out as if pursued by a thousand Christian devils, and raced off into the night, never even glancing at the small group by the gate. The priest and the old Mandarins bowed to each other again in silence and respect, and in the yellow flare of their torchlight the three ancients continued their slow and dignified progress toward their homes.

In the days that followed, the boy fretted continually over the plight of Jade, and could not bear that it was impossible to save her. He tried to question his master on the customs of Christian marriage.

The Jesuit was a little short with his answers, because he was very busy. Now that he could write fairly easily, he was occupied with a plan to translate the Catechism into Chinese; then at last he could reach these people with the written teachings of God. With the exception of the Bachelors of the tower, most of the educated ones honored and respected him, but it was not enough to talk with them. He must place the word of God into their hands that they might read it and talk of it themselves. He was also working on a map of the world for Wang P'an, having been brought close to impolite laughter by the map the Governor had shown him, drawn by his own Chinese map-makers. In this map China occupied almost the entire world, with all the countries of the western world cluttered into a corner at one side.

Thus, with the Catechism and the map, and the anxieties of the mission, his mind was very full, and the boy's questions as to how many wives a Christian might have did not get the patient attention that they might have some other time.

"You have a few years yet to go," the priest smiled, looking at the anxious young face. "Surely you are not going to bring a wife to my house!" The boy could not smile back, nor could he see any real help, even if he did get the priest to understand. Desperately he pressed on, asking what could be done if a Chinese girl should be asked to marry against her will, and the priest smiled again.

"She does not want to marry you then? You will drag her here by the hair?"

His face sobered then, and he spoke sadly of the Chinese attitude that women were like the animals of the house, to be disposed of as seemed best, without any thought that they were people.

"That is what I mean," the boy cried eagerly, and the Jesuit shrugged.

"We must walk before we can run," he said carefully, as if to himself. "Let us first get even one Christian thought firmly planted in the Chinese mind, and I will feel we have made progress. It will be for those who come after me, and even after that, to think about their laws and customs."

Both the Jesuit and the boy were so sunk in their own preoccupations that they paid little heed to what was going on in town, and the boy was only roused to it abruptly one day, when a clod of earth struck him on the side of the head as he walked along the street. It was followed by a torrent of abuse in the coarsest Cantonese, cursing him for a treacherous Chinese, willing servant to a barbarian foreigner who was planning to destroy China. He paid more attention that day to what was going on about him, instead of walking in a haze of misery about the girl. He listened to the conversations in the bazaars, and met the openly hostile glances in the streets, and what he heard and saw sent him flying home to the mission, his sandals whipping up the first dust of the dry season.

"Honored Father!" he burst out, with no courtesy, and the priest looked up, startled, from his work. "Honored Father, do you know what they are saying in the bazaars?"

Father Ricci was calm.

181

"They are always saying something in the bazaars. What now?"

"This boy that you shut up the other night! Honored Father, they are saying that you had this youth locked away for days, and that you had filled him with opium and would have sold him for a slave in Macao, if his friends had not rescued him. They have laid a formal complaint against you with the Governor!"

The priest stared at him in astonishment.

"But that is nonsense, idle talk. They cannot prove it, and those old men know that he was here only a couple of hours. Naturally I was angry!"

"Yes, master," the boy said. "They know. But who were these ancients? Can we find them?"

Now Father Ricci looked seriously at the boy, and down at the careful brushwork of his Catechism. Dear God, was it all to go for nothing, because of some lying, ignorant, hostility?

"No," he said then, heavily, to the waiting child. "No, I do not know who they were, or where I should look to find them."

They were still staring at each other when the two soldiers arrived in the livery of Wang P'an. They carried a scroll commanding the foreign priest to appear before the Governor at the eighth hour in the morning, and under pain of death if he should fail, to answer charges laid against him by the citizens of the town.

11

There was nothing that they could do. One ancient Mandarin in an embroidered robe was very like another, and in the short time left before the trial there was no hope of seeking them out in the crowded city.

The Jesuit faced the morning with a dark and heavy heart. Tried by loneliness and anxiety, his one moment of short temper may well have cost China all her hope of salvation for years to come; may well have lost him all the fragile foothold that he had so patiently achieved. He was filled with guilt, and did not feel that God could ever forgive him. Nor could he forgive himself. It seemed only justice that the streets were filled with a hostile crowd as he made his slow way to the Governor's House. What matter that they were blaming him for something that he had not done? He had done enough to earn all their hostility.

The Hall of Justice opened out of the Outer Court of Wang P'an, and at its doorway the priest was surrounded coldly by the Governor's Guard, instead of receiving his usual bowing reception at the hands of the Chamberlain.

"Out," a soldier said to the boy, placing the flat of

his naked sword across his chest. "You are not allowed in there. Unless," he leered, "you are a criminal yourself." The boy thought of Jade, and the sunlight almost darkened with his fright. Did you but know, he thought!

Aloud, he cried out fiercely, watching his master being led away from him.

"I must go in!" he cried, "I must! I am the Honored Father's tongue! I have to speak for him when he cannot speak well enough for himself."

The soldier laughed unkindly.

"Today he must speak for himself," he said, "and much good may it do him." He spat sourly. "Barbarian foreigners imprisoning Chinese! Let him taste the closed walls himself for a while, if Excellency does not have him beaten to death!"

The boy could not move against the bright blade on his chest.

"He did nothing!" he shouted. "Nothing! Only what you would do yourself if someone harmed your house! I must speak for him!"

Ahead, the priest heard the frantic cries and turned in the close ring of his guards. He was too far away to speak unless he shouted in return, but he looked at the boy quietly, and held up his right hand in the gesture that even he had come to know meant peace in the name of the Lord of Heaven. Seeing the gesture, the boy fell silent and turned away, pushing the sword aside with the flat of his hand as though it were a green leaf of bamboo. Somehow he had understood that the Father was in the care of his own God, and did not need his help.

Matteo Ricci could do no more than commend himself to his God, for he could not help himself. He was led between two guards as though he were a common felon, down the long floor of black tiles to where his friend Wang P'an sat behind his crimson table in his white-winged hat. His ivory face was chilly and inscrutable, where the Jesuit had come to know its more private look of warmth and mildness, and he looked at the accused as if he had never seen him before. In the folds of his Buddhist robe Father Ricci fingered his rosary, and begged help for the sake of China from the only One that he could think might help him now.

The charge was read by a cold-eyed official, who lifted his glance of hate above the scroll, and put into the accusations all his personal belief that the accused was guilty of everything it said. Then the youth himself was pushed forward, narrow-eyed and furtive, looking at no one while he poured out his tale of the days he had been held prisoner by the foreigner, and the beatings he had received, and the drugs that had been forced upon him to make him unconscious, so that he would have been taken away and sold as a slave had his friends not rescued him.

Before the astounded priest, the friends came glibly one by one, to testify that it was all true, and their description of finding the youth, trussed and drugged, in the storehouse of the priest, rang out so true and clear that the Jesuit passed his hand across his forehead and gazed astonished at Wang P'an, almost half convinced of the lies himself by now.

When the time came for him to speak he was filled with hopelessness by the thorough way in which his enemies had organized his downfall. Who would believe his stammering and inadequate Chinese, against all these stories telling the same facts? Who could prove him right, except maybe those three old Mandarins, nodding over their books and pipes in some warm pavilion, utterly unaware of his desperate need of them? Carefully he chose his words and did his best to speak clearly, telling of the stones crashing through the roof ever since the turning of the year, and of the one single evening when they had been quick enough to catch the culprit. But even as he stammered on, he knew from the growing chill of Wang P'an's face and from the hiss of disapproval around the hall that he was not being believed. He was only adding to his crime by accusing an innocent Chinese youth in order to try and defend himself. He could have wept for his failure; for all that he had accomplished that must now go to waste; for China, which would have to wait perhaps centuries again for someone else to break down her barriers with the word of God. He, Matteo Ricci, had failed, as all those had failed who had come before him.

Outside the hall the boy sat as quietly as he could. For him too, it would be an ending, although he could

186

see nothing but an ending in any case to his secret meetings with Jade. It was like a sick shadow over the bright day to know that if his master were thrown out of China, there would go his last hope of ever seeing her again. It would even have been something if she were in the end closed in the courts of Lu Chin. He would have known himself at least to be in the same town as she was. She had been the only friend of his own age that he had ever had, some fierce dignity always holding him apart from the other beggar children in Macao. For all the brilliant day, and the busy, bustling color of Wang P'an's Court, the blossom and the glittering water in the gardens, and the brightly colored tiles of the pagoda roofs, he had the feeling that his world had grown dark. His beloved master was on trial for his very life, and he had lost his only friend.

Idly he watched a scuffle at the outer gate, someone coming around the screen in most unseemly haste, and an old man too, who should have put more value on his dignity. He was followed by another old man, scuttling along also in his long robes and tripping over his feet, his servants almost running to keep up with him. The boy gasped and then shouted, and was on his feet and running to them before the third panting ancient was around the screen.

"You have come!" he cried, bowing and backing before the first one. "Honored sirs, you have come to save my master!"

The old man showed an instant of distaste to speak

187

directly to so humble a servant, but knew the urgency
of the moment.

"We have heard that your master is being tried for
crimes he did not commit. What can we do but speak?
Make haste boy—we have only heard of it this moment."

It was agony for him to watch them wasting even a
few minutes collecting their dignity outside the great
double door, surrounded by officials bowing to their age

and importance. Then the doors opened and closed behind them, and the boy collapsed on his bench as though he himself were suddenly grown old. They would stay now in Siuching. Maybe he could not help Jade, but he would at least be in the same town and that would be something. In Siuching. Siuching. The very name was strangely comforting. He may belong to the Family of the Lord of Heaven, but now when people asked him where he came from, he was able to say "Siuching."

In her green cotton suit Jade sat down suddenly beside him, and opening his eyes, he stared at her in speechless fright. The suit no longer had the sparkling look of newness that it had on the first day they stood together to look at the prism. The folds of freshness were gone, and the black buttoned cap was battered, the button hanging loose on a thread.

At last he found his voice.

"You must be mad," he said, "to be seen here!"

Jade looked at him, and he did not know how he had ever thought her to have a boy's face.

"Where safer?" she asked him. "No one in my uncle's Outer Courts has ever seen me, and today when it is a Day of Judgment and the people are allowed in, it is as safe as the streets of the town."

The boy groaned.

"Nowhere is safe."

"Everywhere is safe, except in the Inner Courts, where my face is known. Eldest Uncle told me that your foreign master was on trial here today, and I thought you would be with him. I came to look for you."

Eagerly he turned to her.

"And did your Eldest Uncle think him guilty? He was not, and now there are people gone into the hall who can prove it."

"My uncle thinks no one guilty until they have had a fair trial. I can tell you he was much troubled about the bonze Ri-ki, and will be happy if he can find him innocent." She grinned, the amiable, friendly smile that had come through the curtains of the palanquin. "He little knows how much I know about him, and the other foreign bonze."

"Well, quickly! Out with it." He found it easier to talk to her if he pretended that she was still the boy Chang, but even as he spoke he saw her face change, and knew he could not pretend any more. He was too stricken by the naked fear in her face; fear in a girl's face, thinning the round cheeks and making the wide eyes old and haunted.

"I want your help."

"For what?" The small stricken face touched him desperately in some way he would not like to admit, but there was some uproar going on inside the Hall of Justice, and half his mind was on his master. "Help for what?"

"I am going to run away."

"Run away! And you want me to help you! It is not . . . I cannot . . . you cannot!" He could not even begin to find words for the impossibility of a well-born Chinese girl leaving her family home.

Jade drew a deep, painful breath and quelled the tears.

"I cannot marry Lu Chin. I have seen him again through the lattice, and I cannot! I cannot! I will not go to his courts. I would rather die, or be a beggar, and I am going to run away whether you will help me or not."

Defeated, he stared at her. Then relief welled in him to see the big doors of the Hall of Justice opening, and the tall, gray figure of his master walking out with the three old Mandarins smiling and bowing around him. They appeared quite unperturbed by a most terrible screaming that had begun in the court behind them, but the boy turned pale to listen to it, knowing his own future if he were caught with this girl. He did not speak, only bowing low before the Jesuit, his mind all the time on the screams of agony. The priest's face was almost more unhappy than when he went in.

"It is well for us, my son," he said to the boy. "These good ancient ones have cleared me." He bowed in turn to the three Mandarins. "But listen, listen to what they do to the poor wretched youth who was so foolish as to lie to me. They are beating him to death, and I could not stop it. Come, boy, for I cannot stand to listen to it."

Nor could the boy. This was the dreadful death for the simple bearing of false witness. What could happen to him if he helped the Governor's niece to run away?

He almost dared not look around lest the girl should rush up to him, involving his master in her dangerous plan. To his intense relief, she was nowhere in sight.

"Let that be a lesson to me," the priest said to the boy when at last they parted from the three ancients. "Let that be a lesson to us all. Never again must there be a moment of lost patience, no matter what happens to us. God is not served by anger. I should have known that."

His voice was hoarse with sudden weariness, and the breaking of the strain that had gripped him that he had failed the land of China, and failed in the task that his Superiors had given him. Of his own safety he had barely thought at all. Walking in his place a small way behind, the boy could not see his face, but sensed the weariness and sorrow in the priest's voice and rushed to offer comfort.

"It will not happen again, master," he urged. "Excellency has said that you are innocent, and see, the word is already through the town. My people are not cruel; already they smile at you again in the streets, and would tell you that they are sorry they spoke evil."

Looking around him, the priest knew that this was true. With the quick Chinese change of mood, the whole atmosphere was different from a few hours before when he had walked in the center of a hissing crowd to the Hall of Justice. On all sides were shamefaced smiles and respectful bows, and the people stood back to let him pass. There was more to it than this. Wang P'an knew as well as he did himself that you could talk forever to this quick and lively people and they would never heed you. But the written word was law to them, so the Governor ordered his scribes to paint two scrolls to be hung up in the Christian church; one reminding the thoughtless people of Siuching that these bonzes were here under the protection of Wang P'an himself; and one reminding them of the fate of the youth who had borne false witness, and promising them the same agonizing end for the same crime.

Father Ricci settled down to his patient work, which never seemed to amount to anything more than the calm example of wisdom and dignity, and the welcoming of all Chinese, however humble, who came near the mission. They usually came in curiosity, and then stayed politely to listen to all they were told; going away with blank, well-mannered faces, and no sign that they had heard one word they would remember. The Jesuit put firmly from his mind the growing longing to be able to say, "This one man has become a Christian because of me, and of what I have taught." He had the friendship of China, but he had made no Chinese Christians. He forced himself to be patient and to believe that God would bring these in His own good time.

Through these bright days, when the sun glittered on the river and brought the scent of the pine trees heavy and languorous about the mission, the boy knew none of the priest's peace. He lived torn between anxiety that the girl Jade would come to him with some madness about helping her to run away—and sick sadness that she would not. He would have to watch the moon rising to the full for the second time after Ming Ching, knowing that if she had not come to him, she would have been taken weeping to Lu Chin's courts, and he would never see her again.

He would not talk about her to the priest. Painful in his loyalty, he would not involve him in something that might only harm the mission. The pale pinks and whites of the blossom browned and faded on the trees; the tiny court was splashed with the blood scarlet of great peonies, and drowsy with the rich scent of carnations, and he saw none of them. The Jesuit noticed his thinning face and quiet eyes and asked him more than once if he were troubled.

"Honorable master, no, I have no troubles," he would answer every time, hands in sleeves and feet together in perfect politeness, yet in some way withdrawn into his young dignity in a way that he had never been. Father Ricci looked at him, puzzled.

"Do not fret that we are so poor, my son," he said. "The Father Mi-kli will soon be back with silver for us all. We have always enough rice to feed us."

The boy bowed and did not answer, and the priest gave up. What other troubles could the boy have, for what other life did he know?

When the moon was in its second quarter, Father Ruggieri returned to Siuching.

It was the boy who saw him first, standing for one

194

stunned, happy moment before he went rushing into the small house.

"My Father! My Father! It is Mi-kli."

Father Ricci paused for one startled glance and then dropped his brush, ruining the careful work of a whole morning, to rush out into the road, where he could see the tall, gray figure coming down the hill, arms already raised in greeting, and followed by the small, sedate figure of Philip. The passing Chinese still stopped to laugh at their warm Italian greeting, but now the smiles were kindly, and as welcoming to the returned priest as Matteo Ricci's own. They did mad, foolish things, these bonzes, the amiable yellow faces seemed to say now, but there is no harm in them. The news of the return of Mi-kli spread through Siuching like summer fire, withering away all the doubts and fears that had haunted Matteo Ricci's long, unfriendly winter.

Mi-kli had brought money too, for the trading season had been good, and with it the blessing of his Superiors on all that Father Ricci had done in this unending task of bringing the Chinese to an understanding of God. They walked beside the river together in the evening, with the crooked pines black against the brief scarlet of the twilight sky, and the reflections of the round hills lying in the still glimmer of the water.

"I felt they might well be disappointed in me," Father Ricci said humbly. "For have I not been now eighteen months in China, and I have not one convert. They might well expect more."

"Matteo," said his fellow priest, "you have been eighteen months in China, as you say. That is more than any other Jesuit has ever done, and you have earned the friendship of Wang P'an and of the people of Siuching as well. That satisfies them well. The rest will follow."

Father Ricci stood in silence, watching the swift, instant fall of the summer darkness; the gentle Chinese night with the moon halfway to its full, loud with the rasping cicadas and bright with the small, wandering clouds of fireflies along the river. He sighed, knowing that if he had not yet captured China, China had certainly captured him, and that these small, gay, industrious people would forever be his life.

"With the help of God," he agreed with Michele. "With the help of God, all the rest will follow."

The small, hollow booming of the boy's gong called them to their evening meal, and they turned backward toward the mission, the hems of their robes whispering in the dark, flower-starred grass.

"Matteo," cried Father Ruggieri, suddenly and softly. "What is that?"

In the soft, opaque darkness, they could see faintly a white shape lying in the grass a little way across the meadow, and when they reached it, it proved to be the body of a Chinese, even in the darkness clearly starved and ragged; a mere bundle of bones collapsed in the scented grass.

"Is he dead?" Michele asked.

"I think so, but we cannot see." The other priest peered. "Go bring a light."

Philip and the boy came hurrying with lanterns, and in the gentle glow the man opened his eyes. He was not yet dead, but his eyes were dark and shadowed with the nearness of death, and it had already laid its print of sharpness on his hollow face. He looked from one strange face to the other in the golden light and his empty eyes made no sign. At a word from Father Ricci, Philip knelt beside him and spoke to him, putting his ear down to the faint whispers from the shrunken lips. At last he lifted his head.

"He says," he said, and obviously did not think of the boy as he spoke. "He says that he has no name, no home, no family. Nowhere to go, and he dies here since it is here, by chance, that he fell. There is no one who will care."

No name; no home; no family.

Father Ricci's eyes went at once to the boy, who listened to this echo of his own words with eyes as wide and black as pools of ebony, sick fear on his face. In the long, silent glance, the priest read the child's mind, that asked itself was this the end that he too would come to, dying alone in a strange field.

Then the priest turned and spoke to the dying man.

"Tell him, Philip," he said, "and tell him clearly, that he is not alone. Tell him that the Lord of Heaven cares for him as He cares for all His people, who are His children. Tell him we will look after him, and as long as he is with us, he will belong, as we all do, to the great Family of the Lord of Heaven. Tell him urgently again that he is not alone; that the Lord of Heaven never forsakes His children."

He heard the boy sigh beside him in the darkness, and saw the dying eyes try to focus their blind gaze on him as the man understood part of all he had said. As Philip made it clear, they lost a little of their emptiness, and the man lifted one helpless hand in a small gesture, as if he would offer them thanks.

"Now," said Father Ricci, and turned especially toward the boy, "we have to help the less fortunate in our family. We cannot take him into the house because there is no room, so we must cut and gather bamboos and weave him a shelter, in which we may care for him as long as he lives."

The boy stood a moment and did not move, thinking of it all.

"Come," the Jesuit said to him softly. "Is it not the law in any family that the stronger ones shall care for the weak? Now, here in the Family of the Lord of Heaven, is one weaker than you. You would not neglect him?"

The boy shook his head.

"No, my Father, no," he said. "And now," he added, "I know what it means truly, to belong to the Family of the Lord of Heaven. I have listened before, but now I really understand."

12

These were bright, cheerful days for the mission, with the edicts of Wang P'an hanging in the church for all to see, and the silver taels that Father Ruggieri had brought back promising security for a long time to come. Suspicion and hostility had fled from the town, and wherever the priests went now, smiling faces, as open and cheerful as the young summer, surrounded them on every side. Through it all the boy walked in silence and shadow, helplessly watching with every sudden nightfall the waxing of the gibbous moon.

They set to work in the dawn after they found the man in the meadow, cutting the green pliant bamboos from the grove along the edges of the river; planting the upright stakes and then weaving in the soft leaves to make a cool, waterproof shelter where a sick man might lie in peace for whatever time was left to him.

"My Father," the boy said suddenly to Father Ricci, as he staggered across the meadow laden with a sliding bundle of bamboos, "my Father, am I not of use to you?"

The priest looked at him in surprise.

"You know you are of use to us," he said to him

warmly. "You have been my tongue in all the difficult days, and through this long, lonely winter, who else has cooked and cared for me? Of course you are of use to us."

"Well then, master, I was thinking." He dropped his load and straightened, but did not look at the priest, too anxious about what he was going to suggest. "I was thinking that another boy like me, perhaps a little younger, might be of use to the Fathers in Macao. Another boy who could speak Mandarin," he added quickly, to forestall the priest's astonished look. "He could help to teach the Fathers to talk, as I have helped you. More Fathers, surely, will have to come to China."

Father Ricci shook his puzzled head.

"Of what concern is Macao to us now, my son? How do we know what they want? It is for us now to think of our own mission, and with the help of God now, it prospers." A sudden thought struck him and he looked keenly at the boy. "Have you perhaps a brother you have never told us of?"

Sadly the boy looked at the ground. He could not explain; he could not tell. The Fathers must not be involved, now that their mission was, as his master said, prospering in Siuching. He sighed, and looked over at the gaunt white face of the dying man.

"The Father knows," he said formally, "that I am as he is. I have no one."

The priest could see it as no more than some nameless sadness caused by the sick and lonely stranger, and he changed the conversation, asking the boy's advice about the building of the hut, and the hanging of the bamboo leaves that should run the water off if rain came.

When the hut was built, they made a soft bed of dry grass and leaves, and spread it with a blanket, and there they laid the dying man, who watched them all the time with astonishment and gratitude filling the shadows of his failing eyes. They fed him and cared for him, and for his few remaining days he lay in comfort, seeing dimly through the summer sunshine the flowers in the green meadow and the far shine of the river. By night he lay and watched, with all the love and reverence of a Chinese, the shape of the great golden moon rounding to a perfect circle.

The boy watched it too, taking his turn to sit beside the sick man while the Fathers had their evening rice. Father Ricci would come then and talk with the stranger, who in the evenings seemed to gain a little strength, as if he drew it from the almost full circle of splendor hanging in the dark sky above the hills. Father Ricci would speak to him then of all the simple and splendid truths of his Faith, for the faint, ebbing voice had begged to hear of them. "A Faith," the man whispered, "that has made people as good and gentle as you have been to me, a dying stranger, must be the Faith of truth." So the Jesuit talked in the luminous, scented nights of the God who came from nothing, and lived and suffered and died that all his people might live forever, and the boy wandered away, for at this time he could not bear to listen to tales of peace and happiness and splendor. He drifted by the edges of the river and sat silent in the long grass, staring into the water.

It was the night before the full moon when Jade came to him. He had left Father Ricci with the sick man, still clinging to life. He did not even hear her come, as he stood disconsolate outside the door of the church. He had wandered in there in the half thought that he should seek help from the head of his family, who was the Lord of Heaven. He had looked at the tiny altar with its flickering red lamp, and at the new picture that Father Ruggieri had brought back from Macao. The Chinese no longer thought that the God of the foreigners was a woman, for they had come flocking to see the new picture, and cried aloud in pleased recognition when they looked at the flowing brown hair and the soft beard. Now they understood, they said! The foreign God was a Tartar! The priests sighed and smiled and let it pass, but woman or Tartar, the mild, quiet face in the picture seemed now to offer no help to the unhappy boy. He bowed politely, lest he seemed to find fault with the Lord of Heaven, but then turned and wandered out again, to stand in the rustling shadows of the bamboos.

She came up beside him silently in the darkness, and even before she spoke, he could sense her misery.

"Jade," he whispered urgently, and in his fear for her, he forgot respect and simply used her name as he would

202

to his sister. "Jade, what is it? What has happened?"

The girl steadied her gasping breath. She had run all the way from the back gate of her uncle's house.

"I have run away," she said, when she could. "I have run away. It was tomorrow, and I could not . . . could not . . ."

In the white, shining light off the river, the boy looked at her desperate face and then impulsively took her hands, trembling in his like captive song birds.

"Do not be frightened," he said, and even as he said it, his heart raced with fear, for what was he going to do with her?

He could never persuade her to go back, to face tomorrow and the courts of Lu Chin. In his heart he knew that secretly he had hoped through all these anxious days that she would come to him. But now she was here and what was he to do? Anxiously he glanced toward the mission. The Fathers *must* not be involved. All was quiet, and the small lantern hanging in the bamboo shelter glowed softly in the shadows of the trees, where Father Ricci patiently made the offer of eternal life to the dying Chinese. Jade was speaking again urgently.

"What did you say?" he asked and turned to her.

"I said I thought that I was seen coming out tonight."

His heart lurched into his throat and he looked at her with wide eyes.

"Who by?"

"One of my cousins. So I am running fast. I dare not

stay—I was coming through the courts of my sleeping room when I met her face to face. I do not know what she was doing there herself," she added resentfully. "I looked at her as if I did not know her, and when she was past, I ran. Fast! But she stopped and stared at me with her big foolish eyes and I am sure she knew me."

"She will tell?"

"She will tell, I am sure. What am I to do? Where shall I go?" He felt her shiver. "They will soon be following me."

He stood only for a moment undecided, with his eyes flickering from the mission to the face of the girl, frightened tears spiking her lashes and her big eyes on him, waiting for his help.

"Have you money?" he asked her.

"I have some silver, and I took some of my jewels. They are my own, so it is not thieving."

"Very well, then. I will take you to Macao."

"Macao?" From the startled look on her face he might have said India, or the far edges of the Western world.

"Yes," he hissed, suddenly impatient. "I cannot hide you here and have my Fathers thrown from China if you are found! In Macao, no one will have heard of you, and I will bring you to the Mission and they will care for you, and no one will ever know."

She said nothing, and he looked at her impatiently.

"Well," he said, "I thought you were in a hurry."

It had all been too quick for her. Easy to run in panic

from all the wedding preparations in the Women's Courts and from the fear and horror of Lu Chin. But in one breath this boy asked her to leave home, and set straight out across this sea that she had heard of, but never seen.

"Have—have you nothing to bring?" she asked, delaying the moment.

"Nothing," he hissed. "Who am I to have possessions? Do we go?"

She took one look upward toward the glow of light above the town. Save for the faint cries of the street hawkers and the endless scraping of the cicadas, the night was silent. No gongs or trumpets of pursuit.

She turned back to the boy.

"We go," she said sadly.

There was no way out of the town before dawn, when the gates would open again in the city walls, allowing the first farmers' carts piled high with produce to come in for the day's markets, their drowsy drivers nodding above their mules. Until then the city was sealed, and there was no escape.

"We will make for the West Gate," he said to her, leading her a way up the gentle hill from the mission. "As close to it as possible, we will hide for the night and slip through when the farm carts come at dawn. Keep close now to the sides of the road, and in the shadows.

As they made their way through the dark alleys and the shadowed roadsides of Siuching, they listened for the slightest sound that anyone was searching for them. But the night stayed silent. No trumpets told them that the Guard had been alerted; no rattle of arms and shouting of orders betrayed Wang P'an's soldiers combing the streets.

"I cannot believe," said Jade, puzzled, "that that cousin would not tell of me. She was born under a mean star."

"It may be she didn't recognize you in that suit."

Jade shook her head.

"I am sure she did." Yet they reached the Street of the West Gate in silence and without question.

"Do not go too close to the gate, or the night guard may see us."

The boy whispered and held Jade back as the West Wall and the high, looping roofs of the gate massed before them in the moonlight, the cold light picking out the curling dragons on the corners of the towers, and glittering along the drawn swords of the two guards who stood before the closed and bolted gate. "Come this way."

He drew her aside to where a small grove of bamboo whispered and rustled under the great red masses of the wall. First they crept carefully around to the far side of it, and then deep into the damp, mossy chill of the space between the crowded stems and the wall itself. Jade shivered.

"It is a place of evil spirits," she whispered, and he was troubled by the fear in her voice. She could betray them both if she got too frightened.

"My Fathers tell me there is no such thing," he said boldly. "The Lord of Heaven, they tell me, protects us at all times."

"This is true?" Her passionate curiosity about the foreign priests overbore her fear, and he kept her calm for a long time, telling her all that he could think to tell her of the many mysteries his masters had tried to explain to him. His voice died in the end from weariness, and from a sudden sick loneliness for his Fathers and for the only home he had ever known. Nor did Jade ask him to go on, huddling in silence against him, with their backs to the cold wall that in the shade of the bamboos had never felt the sun.

"I am hungry," she said after a while.

"I too," he said. "But we must wait until we are away from the town and no one knows me, and then we can buy food. It is an easy journey to Canton," he comforted her. "I remember it well from coming with my masters."

They drowsed and shivered and whispered the long night through, waking from their uneasy dozing to listen to the regular thrumming of the night watchman, counting the hours beyond midnight on his drum. Every time they woke they listened, but the night remained silent and undisturbed, and they heard none coming or going to the gate. By the time the first scarlet streaks of dawn striped the sky beyond the hills, they had decided happily that for some reason, the cousin had not told. In the first gray light, they stretched themselves and hugged their stomachs in their hunger, yet smiling at each other now in the excitement of the adventure ahead.

The first carts were beginning to rumble through the streets of the town and line up for the opening of the gate as they crept from their shelter. But the boy was careful, leading her some way into the streets before he came out into the main street to join the trickle of carts and people. He was quite confident. They could be any two boys, going out to do their day's work on some country farm, to come back at sundown to their homes. He looked at Jade, shabby and inconspicuous now that her green suit had taken a battering, and damp and crumpled from their chilly bed, and he was very pleased with himself. As long as they had money, he should have no difficulty in getting them both safely to Macao, and then coming back to his masters, with no sad future for Jade. He felt important and protective, and stepped out bravely through the dark archway of the gate, the girl walking at his side with automatically downcast eyes.

The guards who stood one at each side of the open gateway took one look at them, and then one brief look at each other. In an instant, the boy found himself staring out through the deep stone gateway at the bright promise of the lightening day, but held from walking into it by a sword across his chest. Beside him, another held Jade, who gasped in terror, staring down at the bright blade. Behind them a cart rumbled to a stop, and the guards moved close.

"Into the gatehouse, and *quietly*," one of them said.

The boy began bravely, hopelessly, to protest, and the sword moved up to his throat. "*Quietly!*"

Hopelessly he turned and followed Jade through the pillared doorway into the gatehouse, blinking a little in the sudden darkness, but not too blinded to see the bright gold and silver on the uniform of the Commander of Wang P'an's Guard, who bowed with impassive face before the tousled girl.

"My Lady Jade," he said, and his voice was as cold as

the red sandstone walls. "There is a palanquin beyond the other door." Jade turned and gave the boy one long, sad look and made as if to speak, but three guards closed around her and moved her away through the door in the other wall. The Commander of the Guard turned back as the big door slammed behind her.

"Seize him," he snarled, and the boy looked at him and saw his death in the narrow face.

He was not even taken before Wang P'an for any farce of a trial, for his capture in the incredible act of stealing his niece was sufficient for the Governor to order his immediate death. But curious, when he heard where the boy came from, he summoned Jade before him from where she had been locked in her sleeping room.

His gentle heart was stricken to see her, small and foolish in her green suit, her pretty face streaked with tears and her shining hair rough and tangled from its pigtail. She ran with her big awkward feet all the long length of the Audience Hall and flung herself on her face at his feet.

"Honored Uncle, do as you will to your wretched and unworthy niece, but I beg you spare the boy. And do not blame his masters! Venerable One, I beg you do not send them out of China. They know nothing of me, nothing, nothing, and they have no blame in this. He only did it to help me, only to help me."

Desperately she wept and the tears ran into small pools on the black tiles underneath her face, and Wang P'an, who loved her, longed with all his heart to gather her up and comfort her, telling her that it was of no account, that he knew it to be but a childish prank. With difficulty he kept from leaning down to stroke the dark head. His household watched, and justice must be seen to be done. Even though discretion had kept Jade's flight a secret, and none had known of the boy who had been taken that morning at the West Gate, he could not let his own people see this unheard-of conduct go unpunished. His face was cold as ivory as he spoke to her.

"Who is this boy," he asked, "who dared to take you from my House?"

"He didn't take me," Jade burst out, and then remembered her manners. "Venerable Uncle, I went and sought him out, and asked him to help me. It was my doing." A gasp of shock rippled around the hall.

"Yet he took you."

"Honored Uncle, I *begged* him!"

"Who is he?" Wang P'an asked again, knowing, but curious as to what she would say.

"He is servant to the foreign bonzes, Ri-ki and Mi-kli, but they knew nothing of it, my Uncle. He would not tell them, as he said they would come at once and tell you."

"This I believe," said Wang P'an, comforted that these clever foreigners, whom he had grown so to respect, need not suffer his displeasure over this. Behind his stern and icy face, his mind was running backward to a day when the bonze Ri-ki had come to him with a young servant who spoke clear, beautiful Mandarin. This boy? A strange, dignified child, with odd, light brown hair that reminded him of—. Mentally he shook himself, and bent his eyes again to the dark head on the floor.

"And why did he take you?" he asked.

Now Jade lifted her tear-stained face and looked at him, and for a second he blinked his eyes against the terrible reproach in her gaze.

"He tried to save me from Lu Chin." In a moment of spirit and rebellion, she raised herself on her hands and spoke to him alone, softly and fiercely so that no one else might hear. "My Uncle," she said, "he tried to do what you would not do for me. He tried to save me from Lu Chin."

He looked at her helplessly, as sick with misery as she was herself. How to tell her that both she and he were bound by the centuries of China to their place and duty as life had called them. How to tell her that things may often be hard for her, but few would be as hard as it was for him now to be stern and cold with her in her unhappiness. He sighed quietly, so that none might see even that much weakness, and beckoned a servant from the wall.

"Go tell the foreigners," he said, "that their servant dies at noon." He honored the strange attachment that these foreigners had to their servants, who meant nothing to a Chinese. "The bonze Ricci may see him before his death. Take the girl and lock her in her sleeping room. You will be punished," he said to Jade, "according to the judgment of your Eldest Aunt, and one week from today you will go as we have arranged to the House of Lu

Chin, and much extra silver will have to be sent with you, for you are even less than before."

He paid no heed to her stricken moans. "No, no, no, he must not die! It was I who did it all. He must not die!"

Nor did he look at her again as they dragged her limp and weeping from the hall.

The messenger came to the mission in the greatest hour of happiness that the two priests had known since they had arrived in Siuching. All that night, while the boy and Jade set out on their small, doomed journey, Father Ricci had sat in the bamboo shelter beside the homeless stranger, his brief spark of life now sinking toward certain death.

In the early day, when the red skies behind the hills had woken the boy and girl from their chilly sleep, Father Ricci came back into the mission and laid a hand on the shoulder of the priest who still slept.

"Michele," he said as his friend roused, staring a little stupidly in the young light, "Michele, the man is dead."

Instinctively Father Ruggieri blessed himself and offered a small prayer of hope for the pagan soul, looking at his fellow priest and wondering why this death should bring to his face such a look of splendid happiness.

Father Ricci looked back at him, and the sun topped the rounded green hills and flooded across the floor, and it seemed as though all the birds in China were singing in the pine trees above the roof.

"He died a Christian, Michele."

Now Father Ruggieri leaped to his feet, his whole heavy bulk suffused with the same pleasure that lit Matteo Ricci's face.

"God be thanked. Our first. Our first in China. Tell me, Matteo."

"You know he asked us for the truths of our Faith, being grateful for what we did for him. In the small hours beyond midnight, he knew himself close to death. He told me he had listened to the teachings of our God of love, and watching us, believed in everything we had said. He wanted to die in the same Faith. I baptized him, and he listened and understood, then he smiled and spoke no more, as if he had held to life just for that moment. Our first, Michele. May it please God to bring us more. Now," he said practically, "we must bury him before the sun is high."

They chose a shaded spot under the twisted trunks of the magnolia trees behind their tiny church, and in the strengthening sun they dug a shallow grave, wrapping up the poor starved body with special tenderness in a bolt of silk and in the cool protection of bamboo leaves. When it was done, the skillful hands of Father Ricci fashioned a small, plain cross, and thrust it into the soil at his head.

"Useless," he said, "to have a larger cross, for if we did, what would we put on it?" He thought of the boy. No name; no home; no family.

"Where is the boy?" he asked suddenly. "His mat has

not been unrolled all night, and I have not seen him this morning."

Lifting his eyes from the cross, he saw the messenger of Wang P'an coming down the hill.

There was little to be said when he faced the boy in his small stone cell. From one tiny lattice near the sweating ceiling, a shaft of sun fell on the boy's light brown hair, and struck the priest with a pang of sadness and memory that this was the first thing he had noticed about him.

"Why did you not tell me?" he asked hopelessly, for about the tenth time since he had heard the whole story, and he knew the answer for himself. In his desperate loyalty, the boy would not risk the safety of the mission, and even now he seemed somehow to have convinced Wang P'an that the priests had had nothing to do with it all. The poor child had tried to serve everyone except himself; guarded his Fathers so that their mission would come to no harm, and then tried to take on his shoulders the hopeless troubles of a young Chinese girl. And all that he had earned for it was an ugly death, which he faced now in this cold cell with the same mature dignity that he had faced starvation in the streets of Macao.

Sick with sorrow, the priest looked at the cool, closed young face and knew that there was nothing he could do to help. He could, and would, plead with Wang P'an, but felt certain that this would be useless. The boy had offended the Governor himself, and above all one of the women of his house. The whole crime was so impossible in the closed circle of Chinese life that it was difficult to believe it, except, of course, for what it was—the vain struggle toward happiness of two children who hardly knew what they did. Wang P'an would say they knew well what they did, and that in the circumstances, beheading was an easy death.

In this lonely last few minutes, there was only one comfort the priest could think to offer him.

"My son," he said, "the man we picked up in the field died during the night." The boy looked as though he found him fortunate, and Father Ricci pressed on to the important thing. "He died a Christian," he said, "believing in all we taught him, and asking in the end for baptism. Can you not, my son, believe in all we have taught you, and die in God's hands as did this stranger?"

Calmly the boy looked at him, his handsome young face pale in the shadows, but showing no other distress. He put his hands in his sleeves and bowed politely, and then sighed a little.

"Honored Father," he said, "I am privileged that you offer me death as one of you. And I think as the man who died, that your Faith is great and good that it teaches you such kindness as you have shown to me. But my Father, there is so much of it that I do not understand. I would be happy to be sure of seeing the Eldest of the Family of the Lord of Heaven face to face, in this other world you speak of, but my Father, I do not understand." He added then, and there was no self-pity in his voice, "It may be that had I a few more years given to me, I might have understood it all. I thank my Father, and will go to whatever Ancestors may be waiting for me." He bowed again with the utmost politeness.

The priest could barely look at him, facing the honesty that even though he would die for them, he could not die a Christian. In a moment the boy spoke again, his hands fumbling at his neck.

"My Father has known that I have always worn my birth chain, sacred even against thieves and the starving. In this moment, I will give it to you, begging you to remember your servant."

With a little difficulty he took the chain from his neck and handed it to the priest, who turned it over, looking at the date of his birth on one side and the good luck charm on the other; wondering once more why there was no indication of his family. It felt warm and heavy on his reluctant hand, and he searched in desperation for anything more there might be to say. There was nothing. The silence lengthened intolerably, until the priest moved over to the boy.

"I am going, my son," he said, and the boy nodded and did not speak, standing with immense and effortless dignity to say his farewell. Father Ricci lifted his hand and made the Sign of the Cross on the forehead above the calm face, thinking as he did so that he had never seen the boy look more unchangeably Chinese. At the door he turned for one moment and looked back. The boy was bent in the deepest and most respectful bow, the sun through the lattice on his light brown hair.

As Father Ricci had expected, Wang P'an was courteous but unshakable. He agreed that the boy's act in no way involved the foreign priests and he did not hold them responsible. He was grieved, and Father Ricci believed him when he said it, to bring unhappiness to their small home by the execution of their servant. But the thing had been done, and no more could be said of it.

The priest could not but see the wisdom and good sense of this, and that Wang P'an, in his lights of justice, had done as much as he was able. He fell silent, still kneeling there before the Governor for he had not been asked to rise. Searching hopelessly for anything more he might say, and knowing the sun to be traveling remorselessly toward noon, he let the silver chain that he still held go sliding through his fingers, as if he hoped to gain from it some thought that might touch this cold ivory face above his head.

Suddenly Wang P'an spoke with unaccustomed sharpness.

"How did you come by that chain?" Now there was anger and accusation and the priest looked up, startled.

"My servant gave it to me, that I might remember him when he is dead. As long as I have known him, he has worn it around his neck. It is his birth chain."

Wang P'an did not speak, but held out a hand, and a servant leaped forward to take the chain from the Jesuit and give it to him. The priest stared at him, trying to read the shattered expression on his face as he turned the chain over and over. Then, still with the same incredulous expression, he pressed some secret spring along

the edges of the medallion, and they slid apart, showing more carving on the inside of the two halves. Then
and only then he looked with wide, astonished eyes at the
priest, all his calm lost.

"It is," he said, "the birth chain of my House." Still
he stared, as though he looked through the kneeling
priest to something that no one else could see. "That
light brown hair," he said suddenly. "That light brown
hair! *Bring me that boy!*"

The servants rushed to do his bidding, startled at the
sudden thunder of his quiet voice, and while he waited
he looked at the priest and then down at the silver medal
and at the priest again. His face was no longer that of an
all-powerful Mandarin, but that of an old man who
trembled on the brink of a happiness he had long ceased
to hope for. When the boy was dragged before him, the
priest saw the effort that he had to make to still his hands
and speak with anything approaching his usual calm.

"Child," he said, and his eyes roamed the boy as if
he would see every inch of him at once, "child, have you
any scars upon your body?"

Instinctively the bemused boy put up his hands into
his hair and rubbed his head.

"It aches, Excellency," he said, bewildered, "sometimes when my head is cold."

Wang P'an looked at him and it was impossible to read
the expression on his face. Then he looked down again
at the chain in his hands.

"You were always an adventurous child," he said then,

and his voice was hoarse and soft. "You hit your head on the edge of the tiled pool in the Lotus Court, running and playing with your father, who was my Youngest Brother, Jang-fu. It was in your second year, a short time before he left my House." He lifted his head and looked all around his Audience Hall, and now his old voice was loud, clear with delight. "There will be no execution to-day," he cried, above the head of the confused boy, who looked across at the priest as though begging him to tell him what it was all about. "There will be no execution today. Rather will there be feasting and rejoicing in all my Courts, for the son of my Youngest Brother has come home. Go," he said, to the gaping Chamberlain. "Go tell the wife of my Youngest Brother that her son is returned to her, and go tell his sister Jade to make ready to receive her Elder Brother."

They rushed to unlock the heavy wooden handcuffs from the boy's wrists, and drew back from him with awed respect, as though he had indeed returned from the World of the Spirits. He stood alone in the middle of the great, black shining floor, still and straight with the dignity that was one of the first things the priest had ever seen in him. Then he grinned suddenly, broadly and delightedly, and dropped to his knees with his forehead down on his crossed hands on the floor.

"Venerable Uncle," he cried, and Wang P'an looked down on him, and could not help but smile himself, his ivory face creased in a happiness that had not been seen on it since the dawn when he had risen to find his brother gone. Love was satisfied, since he had loved his Brother Jang-fu more dearly than any of his family, and here was his son with the same bright eyes and the same curious light brown hair. And honor was satisfied, since the whole family of the Mandarin was now complete again under his roof.

It was some days later that the gongs and trumpets and the shouting guards heralded the approach of the Governor, and his litter came swaying down the tree-shaded road to the mission. Behind him in another litter rode the son of Jang-fu, gorgeously dressed now in crimson silk, brown hair sleeked and oiled under his buttoned hat, but he was nevertheless the same lively Boy that the Fathers had known. He leaped unaided out of his litter almost before the runners had stopped, and was only prevented from rushing to greet his friends by the formal manners that made him take his place behind his uncle. He stood there as the Governor spoke, polite hands folded in his crimson sleeves, but the bright, lively eyes roamed over the two priests with pleasure and affection.

"I have come," said Wang P'an to the priests who bowed before him, "to give you a gift. There is much talking in the town among ignorant people about this man who died here in your care. They talk among themselves and say that you took him into your care only because he had a jewel buried in his head, and on his death, you cut it out in your greed and kept it."

The faces of the two Jesuits fell. They had not been

out much in the town in the last few days and so had not heard this, working busily on their map and their Catechism, and gathering encouragement and hope from the one simple cross under the magnolias. There was nothing to be gathered from the smooth, expressionless face of Wang P'an himself, but Father Ricci took heart from the beaming face of the boy behind his shoulder. He must remember his name, Wang-fu, for he could not now call him "Boy." Truly there did not seem to be trouble behind that smile.

Matteo Ricci began to speak, but the Governor held up an imperious hand.

"I hear these things," he said, "but I do not listen, since I hear very different things from my nephew Wang-fu, who was with you at this time." He allowed himself one proud, contented glance at the handsome boy, who bowed immediately, his face straightened and as calm as his uncle's.

"He has told me," went on Wang P'an, "how you cared even unto death for this homeless stranger, just as you cared for him himself, when he was without his family. I think the same as the dead man said in his sickness; that there must be much good in a religion such as yours, that teaches men to love and care for each other without hope of gain."

He turned and beckoned two servants, who carried bundles wrapped in blue silk.

"I bade my scribes," he said, "to paint you two tablets that you may put on the walls of your temple, and all

men looking at them will know what I think of you."
The two servants carefully shed the wrappings, and the
priests gasped with pleasure at the beauty of the gilded
and enameled tablets, shimmering with the freshness and
delicacy of their new color.

The first, Wang P'an told them, was in honor of the
Lady Mother of the Lord of Heaven whom he knew they
revered so deeply. It was a name to place on the door of
their temple. Father Ricci looked at it.

"The Pagoda of the Flower of Saints."

He could not speak. Thus came about all that he had
hoped for. Into their own words and their own image,
the Chinese had taken and understood his God and His
Church and His Blessed Mother.

Wang P'an turned to the second servant and took the
other tablet, laced with the brightness of gold.

"They came from the West," it said, "to bring us para-
dise."

The Jesuits did their best to speak their thanks, but
Wang P'an waved them away.

"You will do much for our people," he said, "and I
would have them understand."

With infinite tact and courtesy, Wang P'an moved over
then and asked Father Ruggieri to do him the honor of
showing him something in the church, thereby freeing
the boy Wang-fu to speak to Matteo Ricci, for while his
uncle was there it would not have been proper for him to
talk.

They looked at each other a smiling moment, and then

the young noble in the gorgeous gown of crimson silk put his hands into his sleeves and bowed before the bonze in his gray robes, exactly as though he was still his servant. In his eyes when he raised his head was all the love and gratitude that he could find no words for—for this gentle man who had held him from starvation and death.

The Jesuit tried to help him ease the moment, as touched and happy as he was himself.

"Well, my young lord, Wang-fu," he said. "Now you have a name and a home and a family! And a younger sister."

The boy's face broke up immediately into a smile of pure pleasure.

"It will please my Father to hear," he said, "that my venerable uncle persuaded the merchant Lu Chin that my little sister was a girl of such poor behavior that he could not insult him by offering her in marriage. The marriage, my Father, will not happen. Jade will stay a while yet in the courts of my mother. And then there will be no Lu Chin," he added in sudden anger.

"My Father," he added after a moment, "as you say, I have now my name and my home and my family. But I do not forget the long time that I have had no family save the Family of the Lord of Heaven. I have been granted, master," he said, forgetting his crimson robe and his velvet shoes and his buttoned cap of rank, "I have been granted these longer years, and now it may be that there will be time for me to understand these things, and it may be that in my House when I am grown, the Family of Wang-fu and the Family of the Lord of Heaven may be all the same. Is that how it is, master?"

"That is how it is, Wang-fu," the priest said gravely,

and in their silence Wang P'an came out of the church and called for his litter.

The booming and shouting and trumpeting died away up the hill, and Matteo Ricci watched the bright procession fade from sight. Then he turned and stood awhile in the mossy shadow of the pine trees, looking at the two brilliant tablets hanging on the sides of the church door, and from them he looked over to the one solitary grave with its Christian cross.

He did not waste many minutes thanking God. The best thanks he could offer would be to turn with all speed to the next task in hand, and the brush was waiting beside the pages of his Catechism. The calculations of the map were giving him a little trouble; and when the Catechism was done, it would be surely fruitful to start on a translation of the Gospels.

Author's Note

This story concerns itself only with the earliest and simplest stages of the career of Father Matteo Ricci in China, but it may be of interest to the reader to know something of his later life. In 1589 he was expelled from Siuching by a hostile Viceroy, but his mission was now too deep-rooted to be destroyed. He traveled to many of the larger Chinese cities, meeting usually with friendship and interest, for he had caught the minds of the educated people of China, exactly as he had wished, but his heart was set on the ultimate goal of gaining entry to Peking. This he did at the summons of the Emperor in 1601, and it was in this city that he spent his last nine years, making an immense impression with his knowledge of the sciences and of mathematics, and becoming ultimately Court Astronomer to the Emperor of China. Through these interests he carefully led the Chinese to the true knowledge of God, and knew great success with the little Catechism which he wrote in Siuching, and which was enlarged to become the manual for missionaries throughout the Far East. When he died, Chinese opinion of him was so high that at the command of the Emperor he was given a state funeral.

One of the most important things about Father Ricci was that despite his immense work for China, and the undisputed fact that he prepared all the Far East for missionaries yet to come, the history of his work was overshadowed for centuries by a bitter argument over his methods. On two points he suffered the disapproval of the Church. One was the use of "Lord of Heaven" in Chinese, as a title to denote God. Many Churchmen felt that this applied only to the Chinese conception of a half magical spirit. The second, and fiercer, argument concerned the fact that he allowed Christian Chinese to continue their rites of ancestor worship, and to honor the sage Confucius. Ricci permitted these on the grounds that he found in them no religious significance whatever, but the Church disagreed with him, and after the most bitter controversy a Papal Bull in 1712 decreed that he was wrong in the eyes of the Church. After a long lapse of time the question was reopened, but the Papal Decree that cleared his name and approved his methods did not come until 1939, 329 years after Father Ricci's death.

Madeleine Polland

About the Author

MADELEINE POLLAND was born in County Cork, Ireland, but she grew up in a small town in Hertfordshire, England, the youngest of five children in an "eventful yet uneventful rough and tumble family with all the freedom and pleasure of country life available."

Her early interest was a career as a painter, but family circumstances changed her decision. During World War II, she served with the W.A.A.F., in Ground Controlled Interception on the south coast of England. Mrs. Polland married shortly after the war, but it was not until 1958 when her children had reached a manageable age, that a friend suggested she begin writing books.

"I have always been deeply aware of the reality of history, and conscious of the people who made it," Mrs. Polland says. All of her books have reflected this interest, and two of them received honor awards by the New York *Herald Tribune* Spring Children's Book Festival.

Mrs. Polland lives in Hertfordshire with her husband, who is with the University of London, and two children, Charlotte and Fergus.

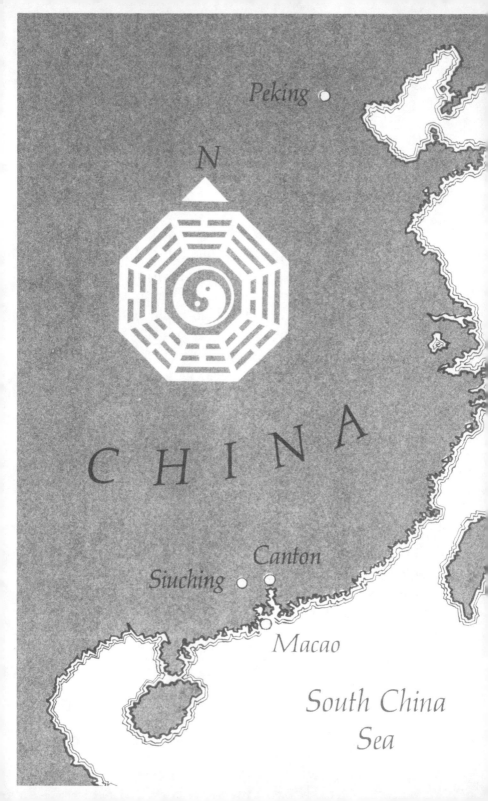